ATTICUS CLAW

Jennifer Gray is a barrister, so she knows how to spot a cat burglar when she sees one, especially when he's a large tabby with a chewed ear and a handkerchief round his neck that says Atticus Claw. Jennifer's other books include *Guinea Pigs Online*, a comedy series co-written with Amanda Swift and published by Quercus, and *Chicken Mission*, her brand new series for Faber. Jennifer lives in London and Scotland with her husband and four children, and, of course, Henry, a friendly but enigmatic cat.

By the same author

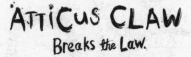

ATTICUS CLAW
Breaks the Law.

ATTICUS CLAW
Settles a Score

ATTICUS CLAW
Lends a Paw

ATTICUS CLAW
Goes Ashore

ATTICUS CLAW
Learns to Draw

JENNIFER GRAY

'ATTICUS
CLAW'

Learns
to Draw

FABER & FABER

First published in 2014
by Faber and Faber Limited
Bloomsbury House, 74–77 Great Russell Street,
London WC1B 3DA

Designed and typeset by Crow Books
Printed in England by CPI Group (UK) Ltd, Croydon, CR0 4YY

A CIP record for this book
is available from the British Library

ISBN 978–0–571–30533–9

6 8 10 9 7 5

To Richard
with special thanks to Alice and Henry

Atticus Grammaticus Cattypuss Claw – once the world's greatest cat burglar and now its best-ever police-cat – was lying in his basket at home in the kitchen at number 2 Blossom Crescent when the adventure began. Of course, it didn't feel like the start of an adventure at the time. It felt like any other Saturday morning. Inspector Cheddar was standing at the back door, brushing cat hairs off his police uniform and grumbling to himself. Mrs Cheddar was frying sausages for breakfast. And the children, Callie and Michael, were making plans for the day.

'What do you want to do?' Michael asked his sister.

'We could go and see Mr and Mrs Tucker,' Callie

suggested. 'Mr Tucker might take us out on his boat.'

Mr Tucker was a fisherman. He had a big beard-jumper (which was a sort of beard and a jumper all mixed up in one), and a wooden leg from the time a giant lobster had clipped the real one off when he was a pirate. Mrs Tucker was the family's childminder. She was also a secret agent, named Agent Whelk. They lived in a big house called Toffly Hall.

That sounds like a good idea, thought Atticus. He liked visiting the Tuckers. He could catch up with his friend Bones, Mr Tucker's ship's cat; and (with any luck) Mr Tucker would let him pick fishy morsels out of his beard-jumper and Mrs Tucker would feed him sardines. A visit to Toffly Hall was definitely worth getting out of his basket for, even on his day off.

Atticus got to his feet and stretched. He glanced at the window. Outside it was pouring with rain. On the other paw, Atticus decided, it might be better just to stay at home and relax. He lay down again.

'I'm afraid the Tuckers won't be there,' Mrs Cheddar said. 'Mrs Tucker asked if I'd mind if she took a holiday, so I've arranged with work to spend some time at home looking after you.'

'Where are they going?' asked Michael.

'Well, the weather's been so bad recently, she booked them all on a cruise,' Mrs Cheddar said. 'The ship's got a pet spa and everything.'

A pet spa! Atticus thought enviously. *Lucky Bones.* He'd love to go to a pet spa. He could get his fur blow-dried. He gave a hopeful meow.

'Don't get any ideas,' Inspector Cheddar told him.

Atticus's chewed ear drooped.

'Poor Atticus!' Mrs Cheddar said, dishing out the breakfast. 'You work him too hard, darling,' she told her husband.

Atticus looked at her piteously. Maybe if she felt *really* sorry for him she'd give him a sausage.

3

Unfortunately, though, Mrs Cheddar didn't seem to take the hint. She sat down at the breakfast table with the others.

'Hardly!' Inspector Cheddar retorted. 'All he does is a bit of community police-catting.'

Atticus felt indignant. It was true that his main job *was* community police-catting. He spent a lot of time with the kittens from the local cats' home, telling them how to keep out of trouble. He also took them on outings, most recently to cheer up the old people in the Littleton-on-Sea old folks' home. What Inspector Cheddar had *neglected* to mention, however, was that Atticus's other job was catching criminals, including Jimmy Magpie and his gang of black-and-white jailbirds, to say nothing of the evil Zenia Klob, Russian mistress of disguise, and her horrible cat, Ginger Biscuit: the animal responsible for chewing Atticus's ear when he was a kitten. Thanks to Atticus, the villains were all safely tucked up in a very large shark (known as a megalodon), patrolling the waters of the Pacific Ocean, rather than on the loose causing more trouble.

The delicious smell of fried sausage wafted

round the kitchen. Atticus's tummy gurgled. It seemed like ages since he'd had *his* breakfast. He got up again and wandered over to the table.

'Do you want some, Atticus?' Callie picked him up and put him on her knee.

Atticus waited politely. He knew it would be very rude to steal something off Callie's plate so he purred instead, which was his way of saying, 'Yes, I would please.'

'No cats at the breakfast table,' said Inspector Cheddar. 'It's unhygienic.'

Atticus frowned. Even though he had been living with the Cheddars for two years now, Inspector Cheddar still didn't seem to know anything much about cats. Cats were *very* hygienic. Atticus spent ages every day grooming his brown-and-black-striped fur and making sure his four white socks were clean – a lot longer than Inspector Cheddar spent in the shower, anyway. *And* Atticus was wearing his special red neckerchief embroidered with his name, which meant he wouldn't spill any food on his tummy, *whereas* Inspector Cheddar hadn't even opened his napkin and was getting toast crumbs all over his cardigan.

'Atticus isn't just any cat, Dad,' Callie reminded him. 'He's a police cat sergeant.' She thought for a moment. 'I mean, you might as well say no *police* at the breakfast table and then *you'd* have to get down too.' She gave Atticus some sausage.

Atticus gulped it down. He thought Callie was very clever to think of such a brilliant remark, but then children *were* clever, like cats. He gave Inspector Cheddar a triumphant look.

'Don't be cheeky!' Inspector Cheddar said, although it wasn't clear whether he was addressing Callie or Atticus.

Both, probably, Atticus thought gloomily.

'Does anybody want some of this?' Mrs Cheddar picked up an enormous glass jar from the breakfast table and unscrewed the lid. 'Mr Tucker gave it to me for my birthday. He says it's very good with sausages.'

Atticus inspected the jar. It was full of something brown and sludgy. He hoped Mr Tucker would give him something better than that for his birthday, like a jar of fish paste or some sardines.

'What is it?' Michael asked.

'Butteredsconi's Italian Truffle Pickle,' Mrs Cheddar said, reading the label.

'What's truffle?' Callie asked.

'It's a type of fungus that grows underground, round the roots of trees,' Mrs Cheddar told her. 'You use it in cooking as a kind of magic ingredient to make everything taste better. Pigs go mad for it. They're very expensive,' she added, as Callie wrinkled her nose. 'Truffles, I mean. Not pigs.'

Atticus felt smug. He already knew what a truffle was and that pigs went mad for them because once, when he was a cat burglar, he had been hired by a pig called Pork to steal all the truffles in Italy. He finished cleaning his whiskers and looked curiously at the pickle jar. He started. A pig that closely resembled Pork stared back at him from the label. It looked like a nasty piece of chop. For one mad moment Atticus wondered if Pork had started making pickles. He told himself not to be so silly.

'I'll try it,' Michael said. He reached for the jar, spooned a bit on to the side of his plate, speared a sausage and dipped it in. 'It's all *right*,' he said, chewing the mouthful slowly, 'but I prefer ketchup.'

He squirted a large dollop on to his plate and handed the pickle jar back to his mum.

'So what *are* we going to do today?' Callie said. 'We can't even go to the park if it's raining.'

'How about you tidy up your bedroom?' Inspector Cheddar said.

'That's boring, Dad!' Michael protested.

'Homework, then.'

'We did it yesterday,' Callie said smartly.

'What about going in for a painting competition?' Mrs Cheddar said.

'A painting competition?' Callie repeated. 'That sounds fun. Where?'

'Here!' Mrs Cheddar showed them the writing on the label on the back of the pickle jar.

Atticus squinted at it.

Butteredsconi's Italian Pickle Products
proudly present its annual
pickle-painting competition!
For more details, peel here.

He watched as Mrs Cheddar peeled off part of the label carefully with her fingernails.

Mrs Cheddar read:

Are you art's NEXT BIG THING?!
Enter our pickle-painting competition
today to find out. Paint the perfect pickle
and win a visit to our famous pickle factory.
Competition closes 30th September.

'That sounds brilliant!' Michael said excitedly. 'Can we go in for it, Mum?' He looked at the calendar. 'The deadline is next week.'

'I don't see why not,' Mrs Cheddar replied. 'It doesn't say anything in the small print about you having to be over eighteen.'

Atticus was pleased for the children – Callie and Michael liked painting – although he didn't think much of the prize. (A trip to a pickle factory sounded about as exciting as cleaning Inspector Cheddar's panda car.) It probably didn't matter very much, though, he reflected. They wouldn't win anyway. There were bound to be zillions of people entering the competition. But at least painting pickles for the pickle-painting competition would give Callie and Michael something to do while Atticus kept an eye on the weather and snoozed. Maybe if it cleared up later, he could go and visit his friend Mimi, the pretty Burmese, by the beach huts. He prepared to jump off the chair.

'Mum, does it say anything about you having to be *human* to enter the competition?' Callie asked suddenly.

'No ... I don't believe it does,' Mrs Cheddar said.

'Then Atticus can do it too!' Callie cried. Her hands closed around his tummy. He felt himself being lifted into the air. 'Come on, Atticus, we'll find you an apron.'

It didn't take Atticus long to discover that he wasn't very keen on painting pickles. First there was the indignity of being wrapped up in a mini-apron that Mrs Cheddar found in the doll's clothes box. Then it took ages to get everything ready, during which time he had to sit on the kitchen table instead of going back to bed. Finally there were the pickles themselves. Mrs Cheddar sent Inspector Cheddar off to the shop to buy all the different types of pickled vegetables he could find. He returned with jars of brown and white onions, purple beetroot, red and green peppers, soggy cucumbers, even soggier cabbage, yellow cauliflower, broccoli with a blue tinge and something greyish-green and knobbly called a gherkin – all of which, Atticus

11

noticed, bore the same Butteredsconi pig logo as the jar Mr Tucker had given them, and all of which smelt equally disgusting. The sour stink of vinegar and sugar made Atticus's eyes water.

'There we go.' Mrs Cheddar finished arranging the vegetables on a plate.

'Can we start painting now?' Callie asked.

'I think so,' Mrs Cheddar said, laying newspaper on the table so that none of the paint went on the wood. 'Which vegetable are you going to choose?'

'The red pepper,' Callie said. She dipped her paintbrush in a pot of vivid red paint.

'Michael?'

'Er ... the gherkin,' Michael said after some hesitation. He mixed some green and grey paint together in an old yoghurt pot.

The two children began.

'Wait a minute,' Callie looked up from her work, 'which pickle is Atticus going to paint?'

'Atticus can't hold a paintbrush, silly!' Michael scoffed.

'No, but he can use his paw.' Callie frowned. 'Can't you, Atticus?' She smoothed a piece of clean white

paper out in front of him and held out a pot of blue paint.

Atticus looked at it. The paint was gloopy, like the jelly in tinned cat food (although of course the jelly in tinned cat food was brown, not blue). He backed away.

'He doesn't want to get his paws dirty,' Mrs Cheddar said.

'Oh please, Atticus,' Callie begged. 'It washes off, honest!'

She looked so disappointed that Atticus hesitated. He supposed it couldn't hurt just to do one paw print. Besides, cats are curious, which means they like to find out about things. And Atticus's curiosity was starting to get the better of him. What *he* wanted to know was if he'd be any good at art. He didn't see why not. He was good at everything else.

Balancing on three paws, he reached out a front paw and dipped it in the blue paint. The paint oozed between his toes and on to his fur. He hoped Callie was right about it washing off. He didn't want to end up with three white paws and one blue one forever.

Quickly he dabbed his paw on the paper and sat back to take a look at his work. There it was: one round fat pad with four smaller ones surrounding it. His paw print! It wasn't too bad, actually, for a cat. He felt quite pleased with himself.

'That's really good, Atticus,' Mrs Cheddar encouraged him. She rubbed his paw with a damp cloth to clean it. The blue paint dissolved.

'Try yellow, Atticus,' Michael suggested. He held out the yellow pot of paint.

Atticus dabbed again, this time with the yellow. Where the two paw prints overlapped he saw that the paint colour had changed to green.

'Blue and yellow make green,' Michael told him.

How interesting, Atticus thought. He was beginning to get the hang of painting.

He tried again with a different colour. And another and another and another until the whole piece of paper was covered with splodges of purple, green, blue, yellow, red, orange and pink.

Just then Inspector Cheddar came back into the kitchen from the garden where he had been cutting the edges of the lawn with a pair of nail scissors.

'Darling, I do wish you'd use a strimmer,' Mrs Cheddar said. 'It would be so much quicker.'

'I've told you a hundred times, you get a much better finish with the nail scissors,' he said.

'Look at my painting, Dad!' said Michael.

'Very good!' Inspector Cheddar nodded. 'It looks just like a gherkin.' He popped a pickled onion in his mouth and chewed it noisily. 'And that pepper is wonderful, Callie! Very realistic!'

'Thanks, Dad,' Callie said. 'What do you think of Atticus's picture?'

Atticus felt shy. He didn't really expect Inspector Cheddar to like his painting very much but it didn't stop him from wanting him to.

Inspector Cheddar took a long look at it. 'Well,' he said doubtfully, 'it's very *colourful*, but it doesn't look much like a pickle.'

Atticus's ears drooped.

'That doesn't matter, Dad!' Callie said.

'It doesn't?' Inspector Cheddar looked surprised.

'No.' Callie shook her head impatiently. 'Everybody knows that.'

Atticus didn't. He listened carefully.

'We've been learning about art in school,' Callie explained, 'and our teacher says that paintings don't actually have to look like the thing you're painting.'

'What's the point of them, then?' Inspector Cheddar said, baffled.

'The point is to make you see things differently,' Michael told him.

'Oh,' said Inspector Cheddar. He helped himself to a gherkin. 'I don't get it.'

Atticus wasn't sure he did either.

'The kids are right, darling,' Mrs Cheddar said, smiling at them proudly. 'Think of Picasso.'

'Who?'

'Picasso, Dad!' Callie laughed. 'He was a really famous artist who painted people in mixed up squares.'

'Yeah,' Michael agreed, 'a bit like a Rubik's cube.'

Atticus was fascinated. He knew what a Rubik's cube was, although he couldn't actually solve it yet. But what he didn't know was that you could mix paintings up like one. There was obviously more to art than he'd realised.

Inspector Cheddar frowned. 'Hmmm, well, it sounds pretty silly to me. How are you supposed to recognise people if they're all in bits?'

'You're not, Dad. That's the whole point!' Callie exclaimed. 'Otherwise you might as well just take a photo.'

'Talking of which,' Mrs Cheddar said, 'I'm going to take a picture of these on my phone. Then we'll leave them to dry and I'll post them off tomorrow. Don't forget to write your names on them. I'll do yours, Atticus.'

Mrs Cheddar took a thick felt-tip pen from a drawer and wrote in one corner of Atticus's painting:

Pickles by Atticus Grammaticus Cattypuss Claw

She winked at him. 'It looks very professional,' she said. 'You might even win.'

'I doubt that very much,' Inspector Cheddar said.

Three weeks later, Atticus was polishing his police-cat badge in the hall, ready to go out on patrol with Inspector Cheddar, when the post came sliding through the front door and dropped onto the mat.

Callie was first there. Ever since Mrs Cheddar had sent in their entries to the pickle-painting competition, she and Michael had been getting up early to see if anything had come for them from Butteredsconi's pickle factory. And every day, so far, she had been disappointed.

But not today.

'Mum!' Callie shouted. 'There's a letter for Atticus!'

Everyone crowded into the hall. Michael picked Atticus up so he could see the letter. It was in a red envelope with smart italic writing on the front.

Atticus Grammaticus Cattypuss Claw
2 Blossom Crescent
Littleton-on-Sea

Callie tore it open.

Inside was a thick piece of cream-coloured paper. Callie unfolded it and began to read.

Dear Atticus,

Congratulations! The judges have decided that your painting is the winning entry in this year's Butteredsconi's Pickle Products annual pickle-painting competition.

You and your family have won a fantastic, all expenses paid trip to the Butteredsconi Pickle Factory. Please text PICKLE to the following number to arrange your visit.

Yours sincerely,

Ricardo Butteredsconi
Owner, Butteredsconi Italian Pickle Products

'Well done, Atticus!' Michael hugged him.

'We told you it was brilliant!' Callie scratched his ears.

'I knew you would win!' Mrs Cheddar cried.

'Hmmph,' said Inspector Cheddar.

'Darling!' Mrs Cheddar frowned. 'What's the matter with you? Anyone would think you were jealous of Atticus!'

'Yeah, Dad, just because *you* didn't win!' Callie said.

Inspector Cheddar went red. 'It's not that at all! It's just that some of us have got detective work to do rather than waste time visiting pickle factories.'

'I'm sure you can spare a day,' Mrs Cheddar said soothingly.

Atticus was sure Inspector Cheddar could too. There hadn't been any crime for ages in Littleton-on-Sea. Privately he also thought Inspector Cheddar probably *was* jealous because he (Atticus) could paint pickles and he (Inspector Cheddar) couldn't. Maybe one day Inspector Cheddar would learn what everyone else in the family already seemed to understand – that cats were generally better at everything than humans.

'Oh, all right then. I suppose it can't do any harm.' Inspector Cheddar got out his mobile phone and typed in the word pickle.

Somewhere in the Pacific Ocean . . .

Inside the megalodon it was dark and smelly. Two black-and-white birds, one thin with a hooked foot and the other fat with a raggedy tail, huddled together on top of an old wicker basket. The basket bobbed about on the contents of the megalodon's stomach: swashing to and fro gently with the waves.

The megalodon, it turned out, only ate plankton, which was very lucky for the two magpies and the other occupants of the megalodon's stomach – a third magpie with glittering eyes, a green parrot, a large ginger cat and an ex-KGB Russian criminal mistress of disguise – otherwise they would have been digested by now. As it was, they were floating about in a mini-sea of flotsam and jetsam, which had also been swallowed up by the megalodon as it slowly patrolled the deep waters of the ocean.

'Plankton, plankton, plankton, plankton!' the fat magpie moaned. 'It's all we ever get to eat.'

'Not *all*, Thug,' the thin one corrected him, 'there was that herring that washed in two weeks ago.'

'But Jimmy ate that,' Thug sobbed. 'All we got was one eyeball each.'

'Then there was the seal,' Slasher pointed out.

'Don't remind me!' Thug shuddered. Ginger Biscuit had claimed the seal. He still had chunks of it hanging from the roof of the megalodon's stomach, including the flippers. Thug had been having nightmares about it for days.

'And the bin bag full of putrid vegetables.'

'Stop it,' Thug said, turning green.

The putrid vegetables, it was thought, must have come from a passing ship. Pam the parrot had eaten them with gusto. The vegetables made her poo smell even worse than ever, which was bad luck for Thug and Slasher as they had the job of scraping it off the megalodon's stomach walls with an old nailbrush and a packet of Thumpers'

Scrubbit which Pam kept tucked about her for emergencies.

'And that tin of soup. You've got to admit, there was nothing wrong with that,' Slasher remarked.

'It was tomato,' Thug grumbled. 'I don't like tomato.'

'And that barracuda Zenia caught,' Slasher continued.

Zenia Klob had once been the world pike-fishing champion. As there weren't any pike in the Pacific Ocean, she had taken up barracuda fishing instead. Her technique – hanging a line through one of the megalodon's gills with a large hook on the end, hauling the barracuda in and twisting its head off with her bare hands – had yielded plenty of meals for her and Ginger Biscuit, but rather fewer for Thug who tended to be a bit squeamish. Anyway, Zenia kept all the best bits for herself and Biscuit got the head, including the eyeballs, which didn't leave much for anyone else, except the skin.

'Have you *tried* barracuda skin?' Thug demanded of his friend. 'It's disgusting: all chewy, like feathers.

'No,' Slasher admitted. 'I prefer plankton, it's got more protein in it.'

'I want to go home.' Thug jumped up and down on the wicker basket, making it rock. 'I want to go back to our nest under the pier.'

The magpies used to live in a scruffy nest under the pier at Littleton-on-Sea. It was there that they had first encountered Atticus Claw. Jimmy Magpie had hired him to steal some jewellery from the humans in revenge for the deaths of their magpie friends as roadkill. However, from the moment that Atticus had found a home with the Cheddar family and decided he wanted to stop cat burgling for good, things hadn't gone too well for the magpies.

'Shut up, Thug.' A strong wing shot out of the darkness and punched Thug in the crop. The wing belonged to Jimmy Magpie. He was always punching Thug in the crop. Except when he was pecking Slasher on the head. It showed them who was boss. And it made him feel better. 'Your whining isn't going to help. Besides,' he landed on the basket next to the two other members of his

gang and lowered his voice, 'spare a thought for me, cooped up in here with *her*.' He nodded towards Pam the parrot. Pam was perched on one of Ginger Biscuit's chunks of seal meat, picking her beak.

Pam gave him a dirty look, which Jimmy returned.

Jimmy and Pam had recently been married at sea by a pirate captain. Jimmy didn't want to get married, especially not to Pam the parrot. He'd only done it because he thought Pam could lead him to some treasure and then he could get rid of her. She *had* led him to some treasure; only something else had got there before them – a large tabby cat with brown-and-black-striped fur, four white socks, a chewed ear and a red handkerchief tied round his neck embroidered with his name: Atticus Grammaticus Cattypuss Claw. And now Jimmy was stuck with Pam, it seemed, for good.

'Yeah, Boss, I don't envy you,' Slasher said as Pam removed a fragment of putrid vegetable from her beak and gobbled it up. She let out a loud burp.

'I'd rather marry a tin of tomato soup,' Thug said.

'So would I,' Jimmy said. His eyes glittered. 'It's all Claw's fault. This time when we get out of here, I'm going to get even with him once and for all.' His face assumed a more cheerful expression at the thought. So did Thug's and Slasher's. Daydreaming about getting even with Atticus Claw was their favourite pastime.

'Whatcha gonna do, Boss?' Thug asked dreamily.

'I'm going to strangle him with his own tail, then hang him upside down from the pier for the crows to peck.'

'Chaka-chaka-chaka-chaka-chaka,' Thug and Slasher chattered their encouragement. 'That's good, Boss.'

'Then I'm gonna pull out his claws and make a comb to clean my feathers,' Jimmy said. 'I'll make slippers out of his ears and use what's left of him for a nest snuggler.'

Thug let out a deep sigh. 'I've always wanted a furry nest snuggler,' he whispered.

'I know, Thug.' Jimmy nodded. 'I know.'

The three magpies huddled together, lost in thoughts of their cosy nest under the pier furnished with bits of dead Atticus.

'Jim!' A sharp voice echoed around the megalodon's stomach. It was Pam's. 'I thought I told you to fix the crate. It's leaking again.'

Despite Jimmy's protests that he'd rather stay with his gang in the wicker basket, Pam had forced him to share with her an old wooden crate that she had found floating.

'Nag, nag, nag, nag, nag!' Jimmy muttered. 'That bird's driving me mental.'

'Jim?!' Pam squawked. 'Stop lazing about and do some work for a change!'

'Coming, darling.' Jimmy Magpie made a horrible face at Pam, which luckily she couldn't see because she was too busy preening her bottom. He flew off.

Ginger Biscuit paddled alongside the wicker basket in a bucket. 'Anyone want a game of murder in the dark?' he asked. He popped out his claws one by one. POP. POP. POP. POP. 'I'll be the murderer if you like.' He looked hungrily at the magpies.

'Back off, Biscuit,' Slasher said nervously.

28

'Yeah, you can't eat us,' Thug chattered.

'Why not?' Ginger Biscuit asked.

'Because you won't have anyone to clean Pam's droppings off the walls,' Slasher reasoned. 'Unless you want to do it yourself.'

'No thanks,' Ginger Biscuit said. He grinned. 'I'll wait until we get out of here. Then I'll eat you.'

'We'll never get out of here,' Thug sobbed. 'Never. Never. Never. Never. Ever.' Great gloopy tears ran down his cheeks. 'We're doomed. Doomed!'

Just then the contents of the megalodon's stomach began to tip. The bucket and the wicker basket shot backward towards the megalodon's tail end.

'WHOOOAAAAHHHH!' Ginger Biscuit tried to cling on to a piece of seal flipper, but it broke away from its mooring and landed on Thug's head.

'Get it off me!' Thug screamed.

'Vot's going on?' Zenia Klob whizzed by on a canoe – another thing the megalodon had managed to swallow in its travels. 'Come here, my orange angel of darkness,' she crooned. She cast her fishing line at the bucket and hauled Ginger Biscuit on board. 'And you two birdbrains.' She did the

29

same with the magpies, reeling them in expertly. Her gnarly hand reached out and threw them into the basket and shut the door with a click.

'HELP! HELP! HELP! HELP! HELP!' Pam floated by on the crate. She knew a few words of Human from when she'd worked for the pirate captain. She had Jimmy firmly by the wing in one claw, in case he tried to escape before he'd finished his fixing job.

'Shhhhhh!' Zenia whisked them in as well. 'Something strange is happening. So pipe down, birdies, or I'll hairpin you.'

Pam shut up. Hairpins covered in sleeping potion were Zenia Klob's favourite weapon. Even Pam didn't dare risk being on the wrong end of one of them. All the villains huddled in the canoe, waiting to see what would happen next.

The contents of the megalodon's stomach levelled out. An eerie silence settled over everything. But not for long. GLUG GLUG GLUG GLUG GLUG! The mini-sea began to tilt for a second time. They were off again.

'Hold on!' Zenia shouted as the canoe set off towards the megalodon's rear.

Great waves of mucky seawater broke over them. Bits of barracuda and seal rained down. Pam's poo became unstuck from the walls of the megalodon's stomach and covered the canoe in a blanket of sludge. The door to the wicker basket flew open.

'I can't breathe!' Thug gasped. 'I'm drowning!' He stuck his head out and got hit by a can of tomato soup.

Eventually the water was still. The villains wiped the sludge out of their eyes and looked around. Where before the megalodon's stomach had been horizontal, now it was vertical. It towered above them as a great narrow cavern.

Zenia's face twisted into an unusual expression: unusual for her, anyway.

'What's wrong with her?' Slasher asked Ginger Biscuit.

'She's smiling,' Ginger Biscuit was watching his mistress closely. Even he had only seen that expression a pawful of times since she'd adopted him as a kitten. Normally Zenia was hatchet faced with a mouth turned down at the edges in a permanent grimace.

'Ha ha!' Zenia cried. 'It's time to break open the burnt beetroot juice, boys and girls!' (Burnt beetroot juice was Zenia's favourite drink.) 'A celebration is called for. I think ve're home and dry.'

'Myaw?' Ginger Biscuit looked at her enquiringly.

She reached down a hand and scratched him between the ears.

'Don't you see, my magpie-mangling moggy?' she said. 'Ve're free. The megalodon's been caught. That's vy ve're this way up – it's on the end of a giant fishhook. Any minute now and the fishermen will gut it. VATCH OUT!'

Just then there was a nasty ripping sound. Light exploded into the cavern along with a lot of other unmentionable things, most of which landed on Thug.

'HERE VE GO!' Zenia shouted. 'HOLD ON TO YOUR HAIRPINS.'

'WHHOOOOAAAHHHHH!'

The canoe shot out of the megalodon's stomach in a tidal wave of gunk and landed on the hard surface.

'Blimey!' said a voice. 'Look at all this lot! You'd better go and radio the boss and ask him what he wants us to do with them.'

Butteredsconi's pickle factory was about an hour's car journey along the coast from Littleton-on-Sea. A large limo picked up the Cheddars and Atticus at half-past nine in the morning. Inspector Cheddar had booked the visit for the weekend so that he wouldn't have to miss work. He still insisted on wearing his police uniform, though, just in case Littleton-on-Sea did suddenly suffer a major crime wave and he was called back to investigate.

Atticus sat on a velvet cushion in the back of the limo feeling very important. It was like being the Prime Minister, he reflected, being driven in your own limo. He wondered whether a cat could become Prime Minister. It might be another thing he'd be good at.

'There it is!' Callie pointed out of the window.

Atticus raised his head. An ugly green building with a big chimney squatted on a promontory beside the sea. The words *Butteredsconi's Italian Pickle Products* were emblazoned across one wall. Atticus sniffed. Even inside the limo he could smell the sharp pong of vinegar. He didn't really want to visit the factory at all. Maybe he could just stay in the car and have a snooze while everyone else went inside.

'What's that place over there?' Mrs Cheddar asked the driver.

Atticus followed her gaze. Mrs Cheddar was pointing out to sea, to a great grey circular tower perched on a rock about half a kilometre beyond the factory. A few seagulls wheeled above it.

'That's where Mr Butteredsconi lives,' the driver replied. 'It's an old sea fort. It tells you all about it in here.' He reached under the dashboard and

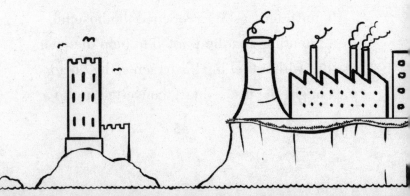

handed Michael a leaflet through the partition.

Atticus glanced at it. The leaflet, which was published by the Bigsworth Tourist Board, was entitled:

The Gruesome History of Sconi Point

'What's so gruesome about it?' asked Callie.

'The fort was built two hundred years ago to stop the French invading,' the driver told her. 'The factory used to be a hospital in the olden days.'

'That's not gruesome,' Callie said.

'This is, though,' Michael read aloud from the leaflet.

Sconi Point conceals a terrible secret: the hospital – once a place of rest for exhausted soldiers – became a front for something much more sinister when the wars with the French were over. A new doctor – known only as X – reopened the hospital, pretending that he wanted to help the poor. But without telling his patients, the doctor bought the disused fort, converted it into a laboratory and linked it to the hospital by a secret tunnel under the sea. When one of his patients died he would whisk their corpse away in the dead of night to the fort and conduct hideous experiments on it . . .

'What sort of hideous experiments?' Mrs Cheddar asked.

Michael scanned the page. 'It says here he tried to bring them back to life: you know, Mum – like in *Frankenstein*.'

Atticus's fur prickled. He had heard of *Frankenstein*: it was a horror story about a man who had made a monster out of corpses and brought it to life with electricity. Atticus didn't like horror stories – they were too scary. If Michael tried to read him one at bedtime he usually hid under the cupboard with his paws over his ears until it was finished.

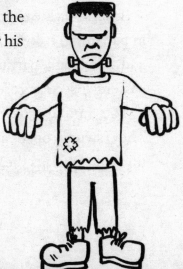

'That's revolting,' Callie exclaimed.

Inspector Cheddar snatched the leaflet out of

Michael's hand and put it in his pocket. 'It's a load of old rubbish,' he snorted. 'I expect the Bigsworth Tourist Board just made it up to get people to visit the area.'

Atticus hoped he was right.

'What a horrible place to live, though.' Mrs Cheddar shivered.

Atticus agreed. There was something menacing about the fort.

'Have *you* ever been there?' Michael asked the driver.

The driver shook his head. 'No one's allowed inside,' he said. 'Mr Butteredsconi is a recluse. He lives there alone with his pet pig and his art collection.'

'But what does he do out there?' Callie asked. 'It looks awfully lonely.'

'Invents pickle recipes, I suppose,' the driver said impatiently. 'I don't know.' He pushed a button and the glass partition between him and the passenger section rose smoothly into place.

The limo approached the gates to the factory. They swung open automatically to let the car through. Atticus heard a clang as they closed behind them. His chewed ear drooped. The factory looked like an enormous prison. He tried to imagine what it must have been like when it was a hospital. He felt sorry for the poor patients.

The limo stopped outside a large corrugated door. The driver got out and held the car door open for the visitors. 'Mr Butteredsconi has a surprise for you,' he said, 'for winning the pickle-painting competition.' He looked pointedly at Atticus.

Atticus didn't budge.

'Come on, Atticus,' Inspector Cheddar ordered. 'Stop being so lazy.'

Reluctantly Atticus jumped out after the children.

'This way.' The driver punched a green button on the wall. The corrugated door rolled upwards.

'Callie! Come and look at this!' Michael shouted in delight. 'It's a ride!'

'A ride?' Callie echoed.

'Yes, come and see!'

Atticus padded after Callie and peered in. Behind the corrugated door was a platform. Beside the platform was a cart in the shape of a gherkin, with three rows of seats.

'Come on, Atticus!' Michael hopped into the cart with Callie. Atticus squeezed between them. Mrs Cheddar took the next row and Inspector Cheddar sat in the rear.

An iron bar descended and snapped into place across their chests. Atticus wriggled. He was wedged in. Suddenly he felt panicky. He wanted to get out! He wriggled some more. The bar wouldn't budge.

'Don't worry, Atticus,' Callie whispered. 'This will be fun!'

'Way more fun than I was expecting,' Michael agreed.

Atticus told himself to keep calm. It wasn't as if he had any choice anyway. He took a deep breath as the cart shot forward into darkness.

'Welcome to Sconi Point,' a spooky voice said.

Atticus looked up, startled. The voice was coming from somewhere above them.

'We are about to embark on a journey,' the voice said, 'a journey which will teach you about the power of pickling.'

'I thought it was a rollercoaster,' Michael complained. 'This is lame.'

Atticus didn't think it was lame. He thought it was scary, like one of Michael's horror stories. He put his paws over his ears but it didn't block out the voice.

'For thousands of years before fridges were invented, pickling was man's traditional way of preserving food,' it boomed. 'Those ancient

methods of pickling have been passed down more
or less unchanged to the present day.'

'Boring!' Callie yawned.

Atticus relaxed a little. He'd got used to the
darkness. He was a cat, after all. And, unlike
humans, cats aren't afraid of the dark, the main
reason being that they can see in it better than
humans can. He took in his surroundings as the
cart trundled along. They were in a narrow tunnel
with fake fibreglass rocks on either side, which
jutted out at angles towards the cart. Apart from
the fact that, as a rule, Atticus didn't like confined
spaces, he didn't feel scared any more. Callie and
Michael were right: it was just a boring ride about
pickles. Atticus yawned too. He might even have a
little nap.

BAMPH! Suddenly a huge lump of grizzly meat
projected out at him from one side of the cart.
Atticus recoiled. BOOMPH! A second lump
zoomed towards him from the other side. They
were being attacked by giant chops!

Callie screamed. So did Inspector Cheddar.

'Imagine you are a piece of meat,' the voice
intoned, 'about to be pickled.'

The meat retreated to the wall. Atticus twisted round to get a better look at it. To his relief, he realised the meat was fake. It was made of plastic. He had to admit it looked pretty realistic, though: all red and gory with a big bone going through it and bits of gristle hanging off.

'First, you would be washed with water.' The voice came again.

FTTTZZZZZZZZZ! Atticus was sprinkled with mist from both sides. It collected on his whiskers. He shook it off.

'Then you would be rubbed with salt.'

A faint dusting of white crystals fell from the ceiling. Atticus stuck his tongue out. Salt. It tasted familiar: he knew the flavour from Mrs Cheddar's yummy chicken gravy. He also knew it from when he'd once swum in the ocean with Bones.

Bring it on, Atticus thought: feeling cross with himself for being a scaredy-cat. He wasn't afraid of a bit of salt.

CLUNK! Something gripped his shoulders. This time everyone screamed, except Atticus, who let out a strangled yowl. He turned his head. A pair of disembodied rubber hands was kneading his fur!

He twisted away. The hands withdrew to the roof of the tunnel.

'And then you would be left in the cold for several weeks,' the voice boomed.

A blast of cold air hit Atticus in the face.

'Until you were ready to be carved.'

A great blade swung down to within an inch of Atticus's whiskers. He hid his face in his paws and closed his eyes.

'Isn't this great?' Michael said.

'It's brilliant!' Callie agreed.

Atticus decided he would never understand humans. They seemed to *enjoy* being scared!

'Now imagine you're a cucumber . . .'

Atticus kept his eyes closed.

'First you would be sliced into thin strips . . .'

Atticus heard the swish of the blade.

'Then you would be soaked in vinegar, sugar and spices.'

Suddenly the tunnel became unbearably hot and smelly.

'Eerrrggghhh!' Callie was screaming in delight.

Atticus felt his eyes sting.

'And placed in sealed jars.'

Atticus peeped out from between his paws. The cart was travelling through a thick wall of glass. It was airless. He couldn't breathe. He couldn't remember when he had ever felt so terrified in his life.

'Until it is time for you to be enjoyed with a burger and chips.'

Now the cart was wedged between the two sides of a giant plastic burger bun. Pretend ketchup spewed out of a knobbly brown burger like blood. Atticus felt sick. He didn't think he would ever eat meat again. Let alone pickles.

The cart rounded a corner. An enormous set of chomping teeth appeared.

Atticus cowered between Callie and Michael. Of course, the teeth wouldn't really bite him. *Would they?* He was so freaked out he didn't know any more. He ducked just in case.

CHOMP! The teeth bit down to within a fraction of an inch of his head.

'And that,' the voice said, 'completes our journey. But remember, the ancient art of pickling isn't just used on food.' The voice paused.

'It is also a way to preserve BODIES, BODIES, BODIES, BODIES, BODIES . . .'

The voice echoed around him. *Bodies?* Atticus thought he might faint. He had to get off. The cart trundled to a halt beside a platform. The bar lifted. Atticus struggled out.

'That was absolutely fantastic!' Michael cried. 'Can we do it again?'

'I'm afraid not,' a man's voice said. 'But I'm glad you enjoyed my little surprise. Most people never realise how fascinating pickling really is.'

Atticus turned slowly. It was the same voice as the one on the ride, only this time it had an owner.

'I'm Ricardo Butteredsconi: Italian pickle giant,' the voice said.

Atticus looked the man up and down and (mostly) sideways. Giant was one way to describe him: gargantuan was another. *Pickles must be very fattening*, he thought. *I'll stick to sardines.*

'And this is my pet pig.'

Ricardo Butteredsconi stepped to one side, his body bulging and sagging like a beanbag.

Atticus blinked. It was Pork!

'Welcome to our world.'

6

Pork! So he *was* making pickles after all. It *had* been his ugly mug staring back at Atticus from Mr Tucker's jar of Italian Truffle Pickle. Atticus examined the pig. Pork was fatter than ever. And no wonder! His snout was stuffed into a trough of truffles.

Just then Pork looked up. A faint gleam of recognition lit the pig's eyes.

'Hello, Pork,' Atticus growled.

The pig's face contorted into a frown. 'Claw?' he grunted eventually.

'Yes,' Atticus said. 'It's me, Atticus. Looks like you landed on your trotters!'

Pork stared at him for a few long seconds. He nodded. 'Like it here; lots of truffles,' he snorted.

Then he turned his attention back to the trough.

Atticus sighed. Pork had never been very chatty, especially when there was something truffly nearby. He was happy, though, that he didn't have to explain to the pig what he was doing at Sconi Point, or that he wasn't a cat burglar any more, or that he had become a police cat sergeant. He didn't trust Pork. The pig might have been adopted by an Italian pickle giant but that didn't stop him being a nasty piece of chop. Luckily Pork didn't seem in the least bit interested in anything except his food.

Atticus turned *his* attention back to Pork's owner. He could see why the two of them hit it off. Ricardo Butteredsconi was basically a human version of Pork. He was hugely fat with a decidedly piggy face. His eyes were beady, squashed back into the sockets by two massive cheeks and a big forehead. His nose was round, like a snout, and tipped up at the end so you could see right up his nostrils, which were hairy; unlike his head, which was bald, except for one greasy strand of hair side-combed from ear to ear. He wore a smart pinstriped suit, a big green apron and a pair of bright red wellington boots. He smelt powerfully of aftershave.

'So you are our winning artist!' Ricardo Butteredsconi advanced on Atticus.

Atticus backed away.

'Don't be rude, Atticus.' Inspector Cheddar grabbed him and lifted him up. 'Mr Butteredsconi wants to meet you.' He held Atticus out to the pickle giant. 'It's ridiculous, isn't it?' He smirked. 'I told the kids he couldn't paint for toffee. I mean, a cat painting pickles! I ask you!'

'On the contrary,' Ricardo Butteredsconi said, clasping Atticus's paw in his big soft hands, 'I don't think it's ridiculous at all.'

Atticus flinched. It felt as if his paw was being attacked by an enormous soggy squid.

'And your cat *can* paint, my dear Inspector. He is very talented. I am proud to have an Atticus Claw in my art collection. He is definitely art's NEXT BIG THING.' The pickle giant waggled a fat finger at Inspector Cheddar. 'Remember, my friend, in art as in life, beauty is in the eye of the beholder.'

49

'We told you that, Dad,' Callie said.

'Yeah, yeah, yeah!' Inspector Cheddar sulked.

He's jealous again, Atticus thought. He slipped his paw from between Butteredsconi's sweaty palms and wiped it on Inspector Cheddar's jacket.

'Where are we, by the way?' Michael asked.

'Under the sea.' Ricardo Butteredsconi turned to him.

'You mean we're at the fort?' Callie gasped.

The pickle giant nodded. 'I converted the old tunnel from the factory into a pickle ride to amuse Pork.' He smiled at the pig indulgently.

Pork grunted. He didn't seem very amused, Atticus thought. But then Pork was never famous for his sense of humour.

'And once a year I allow the winner of our pickle-painting competition to take the ride as a special treat.' Butteredsconi beamed at Atticus.

A treat?! Was he joking? Atticus felt a slight sense of unease. If being chomped by a giant set of plastic teeth was a treat, he wondered what Ricardo Butteredsconi would regard as a punishment.

'Can we see inside the fort?' Michael asked.

'Please,' he added politely.

Atticus peered round Butteredsconi. A travelator led away from the platform into the gloomy interior of the building.

'No.' Ricardo Butteredsconi's eyes became cold and hard, like flint.

'But I want to see the art!' Callie protested.

'Tough,' the pickle giant retorted.

Michael and Callie both looked disappointed. But they didn't argue. Atticus could see why. In Ricardo Butteredsconi's case, no clearly meant no.

'Come,' the pickle giant clapped his hands. His face resumed its benign expression. 'We will return to the factory. I have much to show you. Pork – get me the remote.'

Pork removed his snout from the trough and pulled a remote control out from beneath it with his teeth. It consisted of a slim black box with buttons and a dial with some writing which was too small for Atticus to read. The pig tossed it at his owner. Butteredsconi caught it. He tapped a button.

A second cart trundled up behind the first.

'After you,' Butteredsconi said.

Atticus wriggled out of Inspector Cheddar's grasp and dropped down on to the platform, looking for another way out. He didn't want to get back in the cart. He couldn't possibly go on that ride twice.

'Do as you're told, Atticus,' Inspector Cheddar said crossly.

'He's frightened, darling,' Mrs Cheddar whispered.

'Don't worry, Atticus,' Callie knelt down and stroked him. 'I don't think anything will happen on the way back. Mr Butteredsconi said we couldn't do the ride again. I think that means it only works one way. Come on – let's go back to the factory.' She held her arms out.

Atticus decided not to offer any further resistance. He wanted to get the visit to the pickle factory over with; as far as he was concerned, the sooner they got back to number 2 Blossom Crescent, the better.

He crept into Callie's arms. The Cheddars resumed their seats.

Butteredsconi and Pork squeezed into the cart behind them. This time, to Atticus's relief, they shot straight through the secret tunnel. There was no sign of the meat or the blade or the chomping teeth. Callie was right: the ride only operated one way.

After a few minutes they were back at the pickle factory.

Pork trotted obediently after his master as Ricardo Butteredsconi showed the group through some rubber doors. Lots of people in aprons and floppy hats were walking about with clipboards and spoons.

'This is the preparation area!' Ricardo Butteredsconi's shout rose above the clatter of blades and mechanical squashers.

Everywhere Atticus looked, vegetables were being chopped and pulverised by machines. He trembled, remembering the swish of the blade in the tunnel as it shaved his whiskers.

Their host led the way into the next room. 'And these are the pickling vats.'

Atticus counted six huge cylinders of bubbling

liquid sunk into the floor. One was purple. One was blue. One was yellow. Two others were brown and grey. The last one was a rather ghastly green and stank the most.

'Cabbage,' Ricardo Butteredsconi said proudly.

A cloud of thick gas filled the air as the bubbles rose to the surface and popped. Atticus's eyes streamed.

'Can I ask you a question, Mr Butteredsconi?' Callie said shyly.

'Go ahead!'

'How come you're so interested in art if you own a pickle factory?'

'I adore art,' Ricardo Butteredsconi sighed, 'almost as much as I love pickles. It is my passion. I collect it as bees collect nectar. It is my one true love, apart from pickles and my wonderful pig, Pork.'

'Wei-erd!' Inspector Cheddar muttered under his breath. He went over to examine the cabbage vat.

Ricardo Butteredsconi didn't hear Inspector Cheddar's remark over the bubbling vats of pickle. Nor did the other humans. But Atticus did. And so did Pork. Pigs, Atticus knew, have excellent hearing, like cats. And to judge by the seriously evil look that Pork was giving Inspector Cheddar, the pig didn't like what he had just heard. Atticus felt anxious. It wasn't a good idea to get on the wrong side of Pork. The pig was three hundred kilos of pure lard. He could flatten Inspector Cheddar with one rump cheek.

'What sort of art do you like best?' Michael asked. 'Apart from Atticus's painting?'

'Such an interesting question!' Ricardo Butteredsconi clasped his hands together. 'All art is wonderful. So is all pickle. I collect both. But it is when they are put *together* that art and pickle make the perfect combination.'

'Pickled art?' Michael said dubiously.

'Exactly!' Ricardo Butteredsconi beamed. 'Pickled art is my favourite art of all! It is something very special indeed.'

'Dear, dear, dear! He's as nutty as a pickled walnut!' Inspector Cheddar coughed into his sleeve. He prodded at the cabbage vat with a long wooden stirrer.

Pork's ears twitched. He pawed the ground with his trotter. Atticus stepped out of the way. If Pork

56

decided to charge, Atticus didn't want to be anywhere near.

'Pickled art?' said Callie. 'I don't get it. What's pickled art?'

'I think Mr Butteredsconi might be talking about pickled animals, Callie,' Mrs Cheddar said slowly.

Pickled animals? Atticus forgot about Pork and Inspector Cheddar. *Pickled animals! As art?!* He'd never heard anything so shocking in his life.

'You are right, dear lady!' Ricardo Butteredsconi nodded. 'Please, explain to your delightful children.'

'Well … some artists preserve animals in formaldehyde,' Mrs Cheddar said. 'It's a type of chemical. They use it instead of vinegar. A lot of rich people collect them. Am I right, Mr Butteredsconi?'

'Exactly so,' Ricardo Butteredsconi gushed.

'What kind of animals do they pickle?' Michael asked.

'All sorts.' Ricardo Butteredsconi smiled. 'I have many thousands in my collection.'

'Like what, though?'

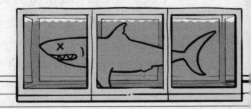

Ricardo Butteredsconi took a deep breath. 'Bats, rats, gnats, lizards, monkeys, mice, lice, spiders, snakes, drakes, goats, stoats, moles, voles, scorpions, millipedes, zillipedes, trillipedes, hogs, frogs, loads of toads, quails, snails, baby whales, sows, cows, bugs, pugs, slugs, weevils, beavers, chicks, ticks, foxes, oxes, germs, worms, bees, fleas and manatees . . .' He paused. 'The art of pickling has been used to preserve animal specimens for hundreds of years.' He beamed. 'But recently pickling has turned into an art form in itself. Your dear mother is right: many rich people now collect pickled animals, especially sharks. They are very valuable. Some collectors even have them caught and pickled specially for their collections.'

'Cool!' said Michael. 'Can we get a pickled shark, Mum?'

Cool?! Atticus was appalled. It wasn't cool at all. A goldfish was one thing but a pickled shark?

'I don't think we could afford it, darling,' Mrs Cheddar said. 'They're really expensive. And it wouldn't fit in the living room.'

Inspector Cheddar was still stirring the cabbage. 'How much do you think you'd get for a pickled cat?' he asked over his shoulder.

Atticus's chewed ear drooped.

'Dad!' Callie protested. 'Don't say things like that. You're hurting Atticus's feelings.'

'All right, a pickled pig, then,' Inspector Cheddar said. He turned round and pointed at Pork. 'That pet one you've got is fat enough. He should fetch a bit. Why don't you pickle him?'

Pork curled his lip. He made a horrible squealing noise.

Uh-oh, thought Atticus.

Pork lowered his head and charged.

'Watch out, Dad!' Michael cried.

Inspector Cheddar's face registered shock, then terror. He tried to step to one side but Pork was too quick for him. The pig's snout caught the Inspector in the ribs and sent him sailing through the air into the vat of pickled cabbage.

🐾

Half an hour later, Inspector Cheddar sat on a plastic sheet in the back of the limo wrapped in a blanket, sneezing. He looked very different from how he had

when they first arrived. His police uniform, which had been navy blue with shiny silver buttons, was now a bright white with black buttons. His face was red from being soaked in hot vinegar and his hair had turned a vivid shade of green.

Mrs Cheddar sat next to him. The children sat opposite with Atticus.

The driver closed the limo door with a bang. 'Can't take some people anywhere!' he grumbled as he straightened his hat and got into the driver's seat.

Inspector Cheddar glared at Atticus. 'This is all your fault,' he said. 'If you hadn't won that pickle-painting competition this would never have happened.'

Atticus felt peeved. It was silly of Inspector Cheddar to blame him. You might as well say it was Mr Tucker's fault for giving them a jar of Butteredsconi's Italian Truffle Pickle; or Mrs Cheddar's fault for suggesting they go in for the pickle-painting competition; or the weather's fault for raining so that they hadn't been able to go out. Anyway, no one else had got themselves knocked into a giant vat of pickled cabbage by an angry pig. Inspector Cheddar shouldn't have said all

those rude things about Ricardo Butteredsconi
and Pork.

'It's not Atticus's fault, Dad,' Michael said,
tickling Atticus under the chin. 'That pig just didn't
like you.'

Atticus meowed his agreement.

'I wonder why it took against you so,' Mrs
Cheddar said in a worried voice. 'It seemed quite
determined to drown you!'

'I don't think it liked Dad saying it should be
pickled,' Callie said wisely.

Atticus purred to show her she was right.

'It's lucky that the kids and me were able to pull
you out with the stirrer,' Mrs Cheddar said. 'Or
you might have been pickled for good.'

Michael giggled. 'Like one of Mr Butteredsconi's
pickled animals,' he said.

Callie sniggered too. 'He might have put you in
his art collection at the fort.'

'Ha ha,' Inspector Cheddar said sarcastically.
'Very funny.'

The driver started the ignition and released the
brake.

'Goodbye, my friends!' Ricardo Butteredsconi

was standing outside the factory with Pork at his heels. 'Good luck with the painting, Atticus! I shall watch your progress with interest.' He waved goodbye.

Atticus waved back without enthusiasm. He breathed a sigh of relief as the limo drove out of the factory gates. He closed his stinging eyes and tried to doze off but for some reason he couldn't sleep. He tried counting sardines but all he could see in his mind were lots of dead pickled animals staring out at him from enormous glass jars. One of them looked familiar. He moved closer to it. It was a human face. He started. The face in the jar belonged to Inspector Cheddar . . .

Atticus woke with a jerk. His breath came in short pants.

'Are you all right, Atticus?' Callie asked.

Atticus purred weakly. He must have been having a nightmare. He cuddled into Callie and Michael: he couldn't wait to get home. He hoped he'd never have to see a pickled animal in real life, or visit Sconi Point again.

Ricardo Butteredsconi waited until the limousine was out of sight. Then he turned to Pork and spoke softly. 'For a moment there, Pork, when that idiot policeman fell in the cabbage vat I thought my dream would finally be realised.' His piggy eyes gleamed. 'A pickled human, Pork! Imagine it! The perfect work of art! How wonderful it would look at Fort Sconi! The centrepiece of my collection.' He sighed. 'Ah well, it was not to be this time. Perhaps one day . . .'

Pork snuffled at him, looking for truffles. Ricardo Butteredsconi gave him one.

'Enough of my imaginings,' he said firmly. 'If I cannot have a pickled human, I will have other great works of art to add to my collection. Come, my pet. Let us return to Fort Sconi. I have a luncheon engagement with some unexpected guests which I think may prove to be very interesting.'

Guests? Pork pricked up his ears. His master never had guests at Fort Sconi, just lunch. He hoped he wouldn't have to share his trough.

The two of them lumbered off and disappeared inside the corrugated doors.

Inside Fort Sconi Ginger Biscuit relaxed on a silk sofa, nibbling pickled rats' tails. Beside him, on a pile of velvet cushions, Pork gobbled pasta out of a golden bowl. Balanced on top of one of Pork's ears was Pam, the parrot. The pig was a messy eater. Food covered his snout. Every now and then, when Pork stopped for breath, Pam would lean down and pick his snout clean, then wipe her beak along the bristles that stuck up from the nape of the pig's neck. The two of them seemed to have hit it off.

Ginger Biscuit let out a sigh of contentment. What a stroke of luck that Ricardo Butteredsconi had paid for the megalodon to be caught so that he could pickle it and add it to his art collection! And that he had invited them to stay at Fort Sconi!

'This is the life, Pork,' he commented to the pig.

'Can I call you Pork?' he added in a friendly way, arching his back and stretching, before helping himself to some more pickled rat.

Pork grunted.

'I'll take that as a yes,' Ginger Biscuit said. Pork was a pig of few words. He was too busy eating most of the time to chat. Ginger Biscuit couldn't blame him. The food at the fort – prepared by their podgy host – was mouthwateringly delicious, especially the rat. Biscuit loved rat (except the wobbly green stomach, which he spat out). Now pickled rats' tails with truffle was officially Ginger Biscuit's favourite food.

Ginger Biscuit finished the last one and looked around the room approvingly. 'You really fell on your trotters here, Pork,' he commented.

It might not look much from the outside, but Fort Sconi was one of the most lavishly decorated buildings Ginger Biscuit had ever stepped inside. The walls were adorned with beautiful paintings. The shagpile carpet came up to his knees. There was a cinema for Ginger Biscuit to watch movies in and a gym for him to do his weightlifting exercises. There were bedrooms galore and bathrooms galorer. There was a library, a study, a relaxation room, a spa, a TV room, a games room, a dining room, a sitting room, a standing room, a lying-down room and a pig room. And he'd only seen part of it! According to Zenia, there was a lot more of Fort Sconi beneath the sea.

'How are you doing with that poo bucket, Jim?' Pam called.

The plush velvet sofa (perfect for sharpening claws) and quite a lot of other exquisite furniture had been carefully arranged around an enormous fireplace full of crackling logs. A decent distance away from the fireplace, a large pile of straw had been provided (for Pork), together with a gold poo bucket (for Pam).

'Fine thank you, darling.' Jimmy Magpie perched on a mahogany table. He pecked at a peach from an overflowing bowl of pickled fruit.

'Doesn't look to me like you're doing any work, Jim,' Pam put her head on one side and eyed him. 'Looks like those two mangy mates of yours are doing it all.'

'Chaka-chaka-chaka-chaka-chaka!'

66

Thug and Slasher were somewhere inside the poo bucket, chattering to each other about how miserable they were and how much they hated pickles. Apparently, even Thumpers' Scrubbit couldn't shift Pam's poo when it contained the remains of one of Pork's meals.

'It's called *management*, Pamela, my love,' Jimmy said patiently. '*They* do the work, I make sure they're doing it *right*.'

'It's called being lazy more like, if I know you, Jim,' Pam retorted. She turned her attention back to Pork. 'Do you want to have a burping competition?' she suggested. 'When you've finished stuffing your face?'

The pig grunted.

Ginger Biscuit decided to move. Pork and Pam had already had one burping competition since their arrival at Fort Sconi and it hadn't been very pleasant; Ginger Biscuit had been knocked off the sofa by a blast of semi-digested spaghetti.

He padded over to Jimmy. 'Having fun?' he asked.

Jimmy shrugged. 'The grub's not bad,' he admitted, taking

another peck at the peach. He looked around the room, his eyes glittering. 'And there's lots of shiny things to look at.'

'Chaka-chaka-chaka-chaka-chaka!' From inside the bucket came a burst of excited chattering. The magpies loved shiny things.

'You three wouldn't be thinking of stealing anything, would you, Jimmy?' Ginger Biscuit asked lightly. He popped out his claws. POP! POP! POP! POP! 'Only, Zenia wouldn't like that. Not the way she and Butteredsconi are getting on so well together, what with their shared love of everything *pickled*.'

Jimmy regarded him bleakly.

'They're both weirdos!' Thug's voice echoed up from the poo bucket.

Ginger Biscuit aimed an orange at him.

'Ouch!' A puff of bright smoke rose from the bucket as the fruit reacted with the Scrubbit.

'Keep your fur on, Biscuit,' Jimmy said sourly. 'We're not going to steal anything.'

'Good. Because if you did,' Ginger Biscuit went on, 'Zenia would see to it that Butteredsconi had *you* pickled, like he did the megalodon.'

Squeak . . . squeak . . . squeak . . . squeak.

'There's Zenia now,' Ginger Biscuit said. The squeaking came from Zenia Klob's wheelie trolley, where she kept her disguises.

The door flew open. Zenia Klob marched in wearing a pair of hobnail boots. The strange look was back on her face. She was smiling. Not just smiling this time: actually grinning from hairpin to hairpin.

'Vot a charmer your master is!' She clomped over to Pork and gave him a thump on the rump. 'Vot taste in food! Do you know vot ve had for lunch today?' She produced a menu and threw it on the table.

Starter
Burnt beetroot pickle with truffle oil

Soup
Traditional truffle soup with pickle surprise

Main Course
Pickled pike's head stuffed with truffle pasta

Pudding
Chocolate truffle trifle with pickled walnuts

Cheese
Italian truffle board with mixed cheese pickle

Zenia Klob let out a contented belch. 'He's a villain after my own heart!'

Ginger Biscuit pricked up his ears.

The magpies exchanged glances. 'Did she say *villain?*' Thug whispered.

'*Molte grazie*, Signora Klob,' Ricardo Butteredsconi lumbered into the room.

The magpies looked him up and down and (mostly) sideways with renewed interest.

'It's Ms, not Signora,' Zenia corrected him. Normally when people called her anything but Ms, Zenia zapped them with a hairpin. But this time, to Ginger Biscuit's surprise, she giggled girlishly.

'So, *Ms* Klob,' Ricardo Butteredsconi bowed. 'As we discussed over luncheon, I wish you to steal some of the world's most valuable art for me to add to my collection.' He paused. 'Ten million euros, Ms Klob, if you and your gang will assist me.'

Ten million euros! To steal a bit of art? Ginger Biscuit's eyes shone. He could *bathe* in pickled rats' tails. He could buy all the truffles in Italy and scoff the lot before Pork did. He and Zenia

could do up Gulag Cottage (Zenia's place in Siberia) to look like Fort Sconi. He could get a shagpile carpet that came up to his *ears*. Best of all, he could travel to Littleton-on-Sea in Ricardo Butteredsconi's chauffeur-driven limo and run over Atticus Claw: *vroom, squish, squash*; backwards and forwards until the cat was flat. Biscuit hadn't felt so cheerful for months. He might even take the magpies with him, he thought generously, to share the moment.

Zenia glanced at Biscuit. He twitched his tail in agreement. 'Very vell, Mr Butteredsconi, it's a deal.'

The two villains shook hands.

'Art?' Thug's face was a picture of disgust. 'What's the point in stealing that? It's not glittery.'

'Nah,' Slasher sneered. 'Not interested.'

'Not even if we let you go?' Ginger Biscuit said softly.

'Let us go?' the two magpies repeated in disbelief.

'Maybe. If you help us do this job, that is.' Ginger Biscuit whispered his plan to the magpies about squashing Atticus. 'I'll take you with me. Back to Littleton-on-Sea. It's not far from here, Zenia said. We'll run him over together and then you can have what's left dry-cleaned to decorate your nest under the pier, except the chewed ear – I'll keep that as a trophy.'

'BUUURRRRRRPPPPPPPP!' The noise came from the sofa. The burp was one of Pam's. It was accompanied by a revolting smell.

'What about *her*?' Jimmy shuddered. 'She's not coming with us to Littleton-on-Sea. I'd rather stay here and let her pal up with Pork. At least that way she's not bothering *me*.'

Ginger Biscuit winked. 'Don't worry about Pam, Jimmy. You and your boys help steal the art and I'll pop Pam in Pork's pasta. He's so greedy he won't even notice he's eating his new best parrot pal. Deal?'

The magpies looked at one another with renewed hope. Maybe this time they really *would* get even with Atticus. And go home too. Without Pam. 'Chaka-chaka-chaka-chaka-chaka,' Thug and Slasher cawed quietly. They looked at their boss.

'BUUURRRRRRPPPPPPP!' Pam was definitely winning the burping competition.

It didn't take Jimmy Magpie long to make a decision. 'Okay,' he agreed. 'Deal.'

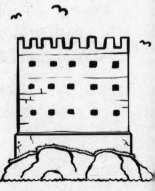

9

INTERPOL INVESTIGATE SPATE OF INTERNATIONAL ART THEFTS!

THIEVES STEAL
MONA LISA!

PRICELESS POLLOCK
PAINTING SNATCHED FROM GUGGENHEIM!

At Scotland Yard, Atticus pawed over a file of recent newspaper clippings. The Commissioner was about to brief him and the Cheddars on the dramatic events of the previous few days.

The children had been given time off from school at the Commissioner's request. He knew from previous experience how good at solving crime they were. Besides, from what he'd learned from his junior officers, they were already involved in this case in a way that he was about to reveal to them. It was quite extraordinary, thought the Commissioner, how Police Cat Sergeant Claw always seemed to be in the right place at the right time. He obviously had a nose for crime. The Commissioner had always believed he'd make a great police cat. What he hadn't realised until just recently was that Atticus could paint as well!

If anyone could crack this case, the Commissioner decided, Claw could. And he had a good team to help him, except for Inspector Cheddar, of course. Cheddar's family were jolly sensible, though, and

Mrs Tucker – aka Agent Whelk – was there to lend a hand. The Tuckers had cut short their holiday at his request; Mrs Tucker was a former member of MI6, the Commissioner had decided to put her on the case as well.

'It's Klob and her gang, all right,' the Commissioner began. 'She's hit two galleries in a week: the Guggenheim in New York and the Louvre in Paris. The operation was carried out in the same way: the guards were knocked out by a sleeping potion administered by a hairpin.'

'But how did the villains get past the alarm?' Mrs Tucker asked. 'Surely it would be wired into the police station?'

The Commissioner looked grim. 'It was. But something pecked at the wiring.'

The magpies! Atticus thought.

'The whole system went down, including the infrared detection device. The first the police knew about it was when the public arrived the next day and the doors were still locked.'

'No forced entry, then?' Mrs Cheddar asked.

'No.'

'Klob probably disguised herself as a janitor,'

Mrs Tucker said, 'and tricked the guards.'

Atticus thought so too. The janitor disguise was one of Zenia's favourites – it meant she got to push a squeaky cleaning trolley instead of her squeaky wheelie one for a change.

'How did they get the paintings out?' Callie asked shyly.

'Good question, young lady,' the Commissioner said. 'They didn't take the frames. They used something sharp to cut round them and lifted them out.'

'Ginger Biscuit's claws!' Michael exclaimed.

'I expect so,' agreed the Commissioner. 'We suspect Klob just rolled the paintings up, put them in her trolley, and off she went.'

Atticus felt gloomy. Biscuit's claws would rip through canvas in an instant.

Mrs Tucker scratched her chin. 'Snatching paintings doesn't really sound like Klob,' she said doubtfully. 'She's not interested in art.'

Atticus growled his agreement. Art didn't fit the profile. All Jimmy Magpie and his gang were interested in were glittery things. And Klob liked jewels too. So did Biscuit. Atticus had never known the two of them steal paintings when he was burgling for Klob as a kitten.

'We believe she's stealing to order,' the Commissioner explained, 'for money.'

'Whose order?' Inspector Cheddar asked.

The Commissioner regarded Inspector Cheddar sourly. Inspector Cheddar's hair was still bright green and he hadn't had time to order a new uniform since he fell in the pickling tank at Butteredsconi's pickle factory. It was dazzling white, as were his shoes and police cap. 'The same man who's responsible for their escape from the megalodon.' The Commissioner paused. 'An art collector by the name of Ricardo Butteredsconi. I gather you already know him.'

Butteredsconi! Atticus nearly fell off the desk.

'Butteredsconi!' Inspector Cheddar actually *did* fall off his chair. He picked himself up. 'You mean the fat pickle fiend with the pig?'

The Commissioner nodded. 'Interpol has learnt that Butteredsconi paid a crew of trawler-men to catch the biggest shark in the ocean so that he could pickle it for his art collection. A few weeks ago the trawler-men caught the megalodon.'

'It makes sense, Dad, if you think about it,' Callie said quietly. 'Butteredsconi was talking about catching sharks specially for his collection when we visited the factory.' Tears rose to her eyes. 'It's so unfair!' she burst out. 'The megalodon wasn't doing any harm!'

Michael tried to put his arm round her but

Callie twisted away. 'You said it was cool,' she accused him.

'I'm sorry, Callie,' Michael said. 'I didn't think about the megalodon.' He held out his hand. Callie took it this time.

Atticus didn't often feel angry but he did now. *Poor megalodon.* It was just swimming about in the sea swallowing the occasional villain. Why couldn't Ricardo Butteredsconi leave it alone? He thought back to their day at the pickle factory, to the creepy conversation about pickled animals. Callie was right: Butteredsconi had talked about art collectors catching sharks specially to be pickled. Atticus should have realised Butteredsconi was talking about himself!

'Are you sure Klob was still inside the megalodon when it was caught?' Mrs Tucker asked.

'There's no doubt, I'm afraid. Here's a list of the megalodon's stomach contents.' The Commissioner handed over a piece of paper.

INTERPOL: TOP SECRET

List of Megalodon's

Stomach Contents

As recorded by

Trawler Captain Jason Squib

One Russian criminal mistress of

disguise

One large ginger cat

Three magpies

One large parrot

Two seal flippers

Barracuda skin (undigested)

One crate

One wicker basket

One canoe

One tin of tomato soup (unopened)

A large quantity of parrot poo

'Captain Squib radioed Butteredsconi and asked what he should do with them,' the Commissioner went on. 'Butteredsconi told him to deliver the megalodon and its stomach contents to Fort Sconi. Approximately ten days ago that's exactly what he did. The trawler dropped the whole lot off at the fort.'

'You mean they were there when we were?' Michael gasped.

'I think so,' the Commissioner said.

'That was probably part of the reason why he wouldn't show us round the fort,' Callie said. 'He didn't want anyone to see the megalodon.'

'Or the villains,' added Michael.

Atticus could hardly believe it. *Biscuit and the magpies had been at the fort?* He kicked himself for not realising. He should have known there was something fishy about Butteredsconi.

'So what are we waiting for?' Inspector Cheddar cried. 'Let's arrest them!'

It was a surprisingly sensible idea, Atticus thought, coming from Inspector Cheddar. He got ready to jump off the desk and spring to cat-tion.

'We can't,' the Commissioner said heavily. 'We don't have any proof that either Butteredsconi or any of Klob's mob are involved.'

Atticus's ears drooped. He settled back down again. Catching a criminal was like catching a mouse: you had to be patient.

'You mean we need to catch them red-handed?' Mrs Tucker said.

'Precisely,' the Commissioner agreed, 'now here's the plan. The villains have already hit galleries in some of the world's biggest art capitals – New York, Barcelona, Rome and Paris. We think London is next and top of their hit list is likely to be Tate Modern. Your job is to intercept them at the gallery and get them to confess Butteredsconi's part in the plan. Then you go to Fort Sconi, arrest Butteredsconi and his pig and recover all the stolen art. Do you think you can manage that?'

'We can try,' said Mrs Cheddar, 'can't we, team?'

'Okay,' the kids agreed.

'Sounds good to me,' said Mrs Tucker. She picked up her basket.

Atticus wasn't so sure. Klob was a criminal mistress of disguise. Intercepting her at the gallery might not be that straightforward. Still, it was the only plan they had.

Inspector Cheddar nodded vigorously. His green hair flopped about. What with his red face and white uniform he looked like a demented puppet. 'Of course we can manage it, sir.'

'Very well,' the Commissioner said. 'There's a police car waiting downstairs. It will take you straight to Tate Modern. You'll be met by one of the curators . . .' He glanced at his file. 'His name is Zeberdee Cronk. He'll show you round. Brief the guards and check everyone's doing their job properly. Then wait. The thieves may strike tonight. If they do, we'll be ready for them. Good luck!' The Commissioner dismissed them.

'Don't worry, sir,' Inspector Cheddar assured him as they left the Commissioner's office. 'I'll take charge. You can rely on me.' He practised a few karate chops.

Atticus exchanged glances with Mrs Tucker.

Usually when Inspector Cheddar said anything like that something dreadful happened to him – like getting cursed by pirates or attacked by snakes. It was just as well the rest of them would be there to make sure nothing went wrong this time!

Tate Modern was a vast, gloomy-looking brick building beside the river Thames with a tall chimney sticking up in the middle and an oblong glass roof.

The police car dropped them on the other side of the river. Mrs Tucker put Atticus in her basket for safety so that he didn't get lost or trampled on. Then she led them across the pedestrian bridge, through the crowds, and made her way down some steps to the gallery forecourt.

'I'll go and see if I can find Cronk.' Inspector Cheddar hurried off.

The rest of them waited. Atticus peered out of the basket, taking in his surroundings. He didn't know this part of London and he might need to find his way round if Klob and her gang did strike the gallery that night.

Behind him lay the bridge, and the river with a walkway all along its bank. Ahead of him the brick chimney of the gallery stretched up into the sky. The forecourt itself was enormous. Hundreds of people milled about. They all seemed to be looking at something.

Outside the entrance to Tate Modern stood a giant dustbin overflowing with plastic bags. It towered above them, the plastic bags whipping about in the wind.

Atticus regarded it curiously. Honestly, he thought, some people were so careless with litter; stuffing plastic bags into a giant dustbin and leaving them to fly anywhere. They should get told off.

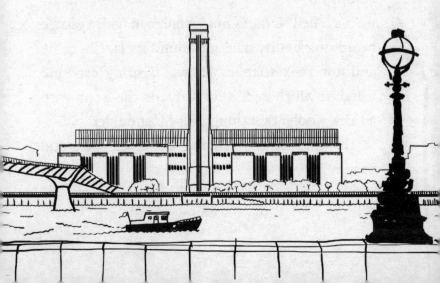

'It's not a real dustbin, Atticus.' Mrs Tucker caught him staring at it. 'It's one of the art exhibits.'

Atticus's good ear drooped. He should have realised that by now, he supposed. If a pickled animal could be art, so could a giant dustbin! And this was Tate *Modern*, after all, which meant it was bound to be full of all sorts of interesting types of art, not just paintings like the one he'd done for the pickle-painting competition.

'Can we have a closer look?' asked Callie.

'I should think so.' Mrs Tucker advanced to the front of the crowd. The dustbin was encased in wire mesh to stop the bags actually flying out of it. At the base of the dustbin was a huge pile of dead fish, strewn higgledy-piggledy on a concrete slab. Atticus contemplated it for a few moments in confusion.

'It's called *Plastic Ocean*.' A tall man with a goatee beard, thick curly hair and round spectacles came and stood next to them. He was wearing jeans and a T-shirt which said 'Kool Kitty' on the front, with a thick wool jacket slung over his shoulders.

'I'm not sure I understand it,' Mrs Cheddar said to him.

'Me neither,' said Michael.

Inspector Cheddar pushed in beside them. 'That's because it's a load of rubbish!' he declared.

'Well, yes,' the man with the goatee beard said, 'and . . . er . . . no. Actually it's pretty clever, if you think about it.'

'Clever?' Inspector Cheddar snorted. 'How?'

Atticus listened with interest. So did the children and Mrs Cheddar.

'It's about pollution,' the man explained. 'The point the artist is making is that the more rubbish we dump in the sea the more we destroy our environment. Get it?'

Atticus thought he did. Humans were really messy compared to cats when it came to rubbish. Everything came in packets and tins and bottles and bags. Michael and Callie knew about recycling, of course, and so did Mrs Cheddar. They always put bottles and cardboard in a special blue bag so they could be re-used. Mrs Cheddar had a compost heap in the garden for vegetable peelings and the three of them used the same shopping bags over and over again. But not everyone did. Atticus had seen a programme about pollution on TV. Lots of people just threw stuff – like plastic bags – away and it ended up in the sea, killing fish.

'Oh yes!' said Michael.

'That's good!' Callie grinned. 'Isn't it, Mum?'

'It's a brilliant idea!' Mrs Cheddar agreed.

'No it isn't. I could have thought of that!' Inspector Cheddar grumbled.

'Yeah, but you didn't think of it, right?' the man said. 'The artist did.' He grinned at Atticus and the kids.

Atticus liked the look of the stranger. He seemed like a *cat* sort of person.

'I'm Zeberdee Cronk.' The stranger reached out a hand and shook the Inspector's. 'You must be Inspector Cheddar. I recognised you by your green hair,' he explained, 'and your police cat. The Commissioner says he's an excellent detective.'

Atticus purred importantly.

Inspector Cheddar ground his teeth.

'His name's Atticus,' Mrs Tucker told him. 'And I'm Agent Whelk.' She pumped Zeberdee's hand up and down. 'This is Callie and Michael, and their mum, Mrs Cheddar.'

'Cool,' declared Zeberdee. 'Want me to show

you round the gallery before it closes?'

'Yes, please!' the children cried.

'Not now, thank you,' Inspector Cheddar said stiffly. 'We're on official police business. We don't have time for any more modern art nonsense. Frankly I can't think why anyone would *want* to steal something like this!'

The kids looked disappointed. Atticus was disappointed too. He would have loved Zeberdee to show *him* round the gallery, especially if everything in there was as interesting as *Plastic Ocean*. He slipped a paw through the mesh and tried to hook a prawn.

Zeberdee Cronk ignored the Inspector. 'What about you, Atticus?' he said. 'Do you want to see some art? I hear you're not bad at it yourself.'

Atticus meowed loudly to show that he did.

'Well, I do,' Mrs Tucker said firmly. 'I think we should definitely let Zeberdee show us round, Inspector Cheddar. We need to get the lie of the land in case Klob strikes tonight.'

Ha! Got it! Atticus leaned out of the basket, manoeuvred the prawn through the mesh and gulped it down.

'Fine!' Inspector Cheddar bridled. 'I'll go on ahead and brief the guards without you.' He stormed off.

'Oh dear,' sighed Mrs Cheddar.

'What are your most valuable pieces of art?' Mrs Tucker asked Zeberdee.

'Well, there's *The Toenail Tree*,' Zeberdee said thoughtfully. 'It took the artist years to collect enough clippings. Or *Mount Underwear* is very popular at the moment. You get to throw your own pants on the pile so you can contribute to the exhibit.' He ran through a list. 'And there's *The Camp Bed*, of course.'

A toenail tree, a pile of pants and a camp bed? Atticus listened fascinated. All of this was art? It made his pickle painting seem a bit pathetic. He'd have to think of something better next time he entered an art competition. He couldn't wait to talk to Mimi about it when he next saw her.

'Okay,' Mrs Tucker agreed. 'You'd better show us.'

'This is the Turbine Hall.' Zeberdee Cronk took them inside the gallery.

The Turbine Hall was very big. It made Atticus feel very small. The gallery was closing up for the night. There was hardly anyone left inside, which made the space feel even vaster and emptier.

'The building used to be a power station,' Zeberdee Cronk explained. 'This is where they kept the machinery.' He glanced around the massive space, a grin on his face. 'It's fantastic, isn't it? Thirty-five metres high and a hundred and fifty-two metres long. Imagine being asked to fill that space with a piece of art! Think you could do it, Atticus?'

Atticus wasn't sure. Maybe he could fill it with sardines? Or a huge comfy sofa piled high with cushions? He wondered if Callie and Michael would help him.

'We could fill it with sweets!' Michael cried.

'Or chocolate!' Callie exclaimed.

'Or toothbrushes,' said Mrs Tucker sternly.

Zeberdee laughed.

'Why is there nothing in here at the moment?'

Mrs Cheddar asked, looking round the vast empty hall.

'There is,' Zeberdee Cronk's eyes twinkled. 'Look down.'

Atticus followed his instruction. Zigzagging along the length of the floor – all one hundred and fifty-two metres of it – was an enormous crack. So that was art too! Atticus could hardly believe his eyes. The crack was surprisingly interesting to look at. *And* it was fun to jump across! He sprung out of Mrs Tucker's basket and over to the other side and back again, purring loudly.

'Atticus likes it,' Callie said.

'So do I!' Michael followed suit.

Just then there was a commotion at the other end of the hall.

The three of them hurried along beside the crack. About three-quarters of the way along they bumped into Inspector Cheddar. He was sitting beside the crack, clutching his left ankle.

'This floor's a disgrace!' he snapped. 'You could break your neck on it. I'm going to call Health and Safety. They can arrange for some builders to fill it in.'

Zeberdee Cronk suppressed a laugh.

Atticus couldn't help feeling a tiny bit smug. Inspector Cheddar thought the crack in the floor wasn't supposed to be there! Inspector Cheddar just didn't *get* art like he and Zeberdee and the children did. He wasn't *cool*.

'What's so funny?' Inspector Cheddar demanded.

'Nothing!' Zeberdee winked at Atticus.

Inspector Cheddar glared at them. He lowered his voice to a hiss. 'Atticus, stop sucking up to Cronk and start doing something useful,' he ordered.

Atticus's tail drooped. He'd really wanted to see the mountain of pants and the toenail tree! And now he was stuck with grumpy old Inspector Cheddar instead.

Mrs Tucker intervened.

'Mrs Cheddar and I will go with Zeberdee to brief the guards,' she suggested.

'Atticus, you and the children find the Inspector an ice pack for his ankle,' Mrs Tucker told him. 'We'll be back in a little while.'

Atticus meowed his understanding.

'Let's try this way.' Callie started off along a wide corridor which led out of the Turbine Hall.

Michael and Atticus trotted after her.

The gallery was deserted. There was no one around to help them find the first-aid kit. All the guards had gone upstairs with Mrs Tucker and Zeberdee Cronk for their security briefing.

Atticus was feeling peeved. Upstairs in the gallery was where all the cool things were – like the toenail tree and the mountain of pants. And whatever the other thing was Zeberdee had mentioned. Inspector Cheddar was so grumpy he'd made him forget what it was now!

A little way along the corridor there was an opening in the wall.

'You look in there, Atticus,' Michael said. 'We'll see if there's anything in those cupboards.' He pointed down the corridor towards a set of double doors. Just before the doors were some cupboards.

'Meow,' Atticus agreed. He wandered through the opening and stopped in surprise. A put-you-up bed stood in the middle of the floor. The sheets and blankets were thrown back and the pillows were rumpled and creased. Beside the bed on the floor were a pair of pyjamas and a half-drunk cup of tea.

Atticus scratched his ear. The bed must be for the night guards, he decided. They must take it in turn to have a snooze when they got a bit sleepy. He thought that was an excellent idea (although he hoped they all brought their own pyjamas rather than sharing one pair). Atticus yawned. Never mind the night guards, he thought, *he* was

feeling a bit sleepy. He hadn't had a nap for hours. He wondered if anyone would mind if he had a lie-down for five minutes.

Atticus was just about to jump on to the bed when he heard Inspector Cheddar calling from the corridor.

'Hurry up with that ice pack! My ankle's killing me!'

Atticus turned round guiltily.

Inspector Cheddar limped into the room. He scowled at Atticus. 'I knew I'd catch you skiving!' he said. 'You haven't done a stroke of police-catting since you got friendly with Cronk. That man's a bad influence on you.'

Atticus felt sulky. Zeberdee wasn't a bad influence. He was interesting and he knew a lot about art. Maybe if Inspector Cheddar had bothered to let Zeberdee show him round the gallery rather than storming off he wouldn't have sprained his ankle!

Inspector Cheddar hobbled over to the bed and sat down on it. He removed his white police cap and white shoes and placed them neatly beneath the bedframe. Then he lifted his legs up and lay back. 'That's better,' he said, pulling up the blankets and relaxing on to the pillows.

Callie and Michael came into the room.

'We'll have to try the kitchen,' Michael was saying.

Just then they spied Inspector Cheddar.

'Dad!' Callie cried. 'What are you doing?'

'Elevating my sprained ankle, of course. It stops it from swelling.'

Did it? Atticus made a mental note that if he ever sprained his paw he must remember to lie down even more than usual.

'But you can't lie there!' Michael told his dad.

'Why ever not?' Inspector Cheddar said.

'Because that's *The Camp Bed* – Zeberdee told us about it. It's a work of art!'

Oh yes, thought Atticus. *The Camp Bed!* He remembered now. That was the third thing Zeberdee had mentioned. He wasn't sure whether he thought it was good or not. It certainly looked comfy.

'Art. Fart,' Inspector Cheddar said rudely. 'If this is art, I'm a banana.'

The children exchanged glances. 'Zeberdee isn't

going to be very pleased,' Callie warned him.

'I don't give a fig what Zeberdee thinks!' the Inspector said. 'I need to rest my ankle.' He regarded them sternly. 'Well, what are you three waiting for? Go and find that ice pack.' He closed his eyes.

'Come on, Atticus,' Michael said.

The two children went back through the opening. Atticus trudged after them.

Perhaps he could have a turn on the bed later. It would look better with a cat lying on it. Meanwhile, with any luck, they might find some food somewhere to keep him going.

He padded off down the corridor after the children and through the double doors.

🐾

Squeak . . . squeak . . . squeak . . . squeak.

Inspector Cheddar was just drifting off to sleep when he heard the noise. He opened one eye and then the other. He blinked.

A wizened old lady was approaching the bed pushing a large tea trolley with a battered silver urn on the top of it.

'Vant anything from the trolley?' she asked him.

Inspector Cheddar glanced down at the cold half-cup of tea beside the bed. 'A cup of tea would be nice,' he said. 'And a Wagon Wheel.'

'I'm all out of tea,' the tea lady said. 'And Vagon Vheels. I got vafers instead.'

'Okay,' Inspector Cheddar felt around in his pocket for some change. 'I'll have a wafer.'

The tea lady handed the wrapped wafer biscuit to him.

Inspector Cheddar looked at her closely. He felt sure he'd seen her somewhere before. The tea lady really reminded him of someone, especially the black teeth and the way her grizzly grey hair bristled with hairpins.

The tea lady was squinting at him too. 'Do I know you from somevere?' she asked, eyeing his green hair and white jacket.

'I don't think so,' Inspector Cheddar said slowly. He couldn't place the face. He unwrapped the wafer thoughtfully.

The tea lady was still hovering. 'You like biscuits?' she said. To Inspector Cheddar's surprise, the tea lady gave him a big wink.

'Doesn't everyone?' Inspector Cheddar replied pleasantly, munching the wafer.

'Vot about ginger biscuits?' the tea lady asked. 'You like those?'

'Not really,' Inspector Cheddar admitted. 'I prefer custard creams.'

'That's too bad.' The tea lady frowned. She leaned in a bit closer as if she didn't want anyone to overhear. 'My pet Ginger Biscuit vould be very disappointed to hear you say that.'

Inspector Cheddar gave her a weak smile. The tea lady was obviously mad if she kept a ginger biscuit for a pet! That must be why she was winking! He decided to carry on the pretence so as not to upset her. 'Don't worry,' he whispered back. 'Biscuits can't hear, even pet ones.' He winked back at the tea lady. 'It won't know.'

'Oh, but it vill,' the tea lady said. 'It has excellent hearing. Haven't you, my orange angel of darkness?' She lifted off the lid off the silver tea urn.

A large furry orange head appeared, its ears flattened against its skull. 'Grrrrr . . .'

Inspector Cheddar's face registered shock. Ginger Biscuit! Of course! It wasn't really a pet *biscuit* the tea lady was talking about. It was a pet cat! *Now* he understood. *Now* he recognised her. It was Zenia Klob and her beastly sidekick! They had come to steal a work of art!

Inspector Cheddar's face turned a shade redder. Suddenly he realised what peril he was in. *The Camp Bed*! That's what they were after! And he was lying right on top of it! He opened his mouth to call for help.

Zenia reached up and grabbed a hairpin from her matt of steely grey hair.

ZIP! The hairpin flew at Inspector Cheddar's neck with deadly accuracy, catching him precisely in his jugular. Inspector Cheddar fell back on the bed, snoring.

Zenia Klob patted her hair back into place.

'Tuck him in tight, Biscuit,' she ordered, 'so he doesn't fall out. And don't forget the cup of tea and the pyjamas. Mr Butteredsconi said they were the most important parts of the vork.' She frowned again. 'Strange he didn't mention anything about there actually being anyone *in* the bed . . .' She shrugged. 'Oh vell . . . ve'll take him anyvay, just in case.'

She checked her watch. 'Those mangy magpies should have disabled the alarm by now.' Just then the lights flickered. 'Bang on time! You ready, Biscuit?'

'Myaw . . .' Ginger Biscuit had finished tucking Inspector Cheddar in. He was wrapped as tight as a bug in a chrysalis.

'Let's get it back to Fort Sconi, then ve can relax with some pickles.' Zenia Klob pressed a button on the tea trolley. Two long prongs emerged from beneath the trolley and slid under the bed. She pressed a second button. The prongs lifted the bed off the ground. No alarm sounded. The magpies had done their job.

'Okay, Biscuit, let's go.' Zenia Klob ordered. Ginger Biscuit disappeared back inside the tea urn with the half-empty cup of tea and the pyjamas. Zenia pushed the AUTO TROLLEY button.

Squeak . . . squeak . . . squeak . . . squeak.

The forklift trolley trundled out of the room and along the wide corridor back towards the Turbine Hall, the bed held aloft on its prongs, Inspector Cheddar sleeping peacefully within it.

1·2

The children and Atticus were in a small kitchen rooting through more cupboards for a first-aid kit when the lights flickered.

'What was that?' Callie whispered.

Atticus felt his hackles rise. Flickering lights meant something had gone wrong with the electrics. Or that someone or *something* was tampering with them.

'You don't think it's the magpies, do you?' Michael whispered back.

The magpies! That was exactly what Atticus was thinking. They had chewed the electric wires at the other galleries in New York and Paris to put out the alarm and the infrared detection systems. It must be them. And that could only mean one thing.

Klob and Biscuit were about to hit Tate Modern!

Atticus jumped down from the counter, trying to stay calm. Everything would be all right. Mrs Tucker was upstairs with Zeberdee and the guards. They would stop Klob and Biscuit from stealing the precious works of art Zeberdee had mentioned like *The Toenail Tree* and the mountain of pants and . . .

Atticus froze.

The Camp Bed!

He let out a yowl. He raced towards the door, meowing frantically.

'What is it, Atticus, what's wrong?' Michael said.

Not for the first time, Atticus wished humans could speak Cat. He tried to think of another way to show them. He hobbled round pulling grumpy faces.

'Dad!' Callie gasped. 'Of course! He's lying on *The Camp Bed*! What if they try to steal that?'

'Surely they'll know he's not supposed to be in it?' Michael said.

'Not necessarily!' Callie cried. 'Mrs Tucker said Klob doesn't know anything about art. She'll think he's part of the exhibit.'

'But they'll recognise him,' Michael insisted.

'They've seen him loads of times before. The worst thing that can happen is that he'll get hairpinned again.'

Atticus had been listening to the conversation. He told himself to stop worrying. Inspector Cheddar was safe. Of course Klob and Biscuit would recognise him. He blinked.

Or would they?

It was then that Atticus remembered Inspector Cheddar's appearance had changed significantly since the last time Klob and Biscuit set eyes on him. Inspector Cheddar had green hair. His face was red. His uniform was white. Atticus felt a sudden thrill of fear. What if the villains *didn't* recognise him? What if Callie was right and they thought he was part of the exhibit? Klob and Biscuit wouldn't have a clue whether there was supposed to be anybody in *The Camp Bed* or not. They wouldn't have time to check with Butteredsconi. They would take everything with them just in case.

Atticus shot out of the kitchen, squeezed through the double doors and chased along the corridor as fast as his paws would carry him. He could hear the children running after him. The corridor seemed to go on forever, like in a hospital. Finally he reached the room where he had last seen the Inspector. His heart sank. The room was empty. There was no bed, no pyjamas, no half-empty cup of tea and no Inspector Cheddar. All that remained were a hairpin and a wafer biscuit wrapper.

Squeak . . . squeak . . . squeak . . . squeak.

Atticus pricked up his ears. The noise was coming from the direction of the Turbine Hall. *Zenia!* He raced off. Maybe there was still time to save the Inspector. The thieves would have to take the camp bed out through the main doors to a getaway vehicle. If Atticus could create a diversion – even for a little while – it might be enough time for Mrs Tucker and Zeberdee to work out something was wrong and come to the rescue with the security guards. He reached the entrance to the Turbine Hall. Atticus flattened himself against the wall and peeped inside.

At the far end of the hall he could see Zenia. She

was dressed as a tea lady. She seemed to be operating some kind of forklift tea trolley. Balanced on its prongs was the camp bed, with Inspector Cheddar tucked snugly into it.

'You were right, Callie!' Michael crouched down beside Atticus. His face was white. 'They've taken Dad!'

The trolley trundled to a halt beside the crack.

'They're stuck!' Callie crouched next to her brother. She gave a sigh of relief.

For one brief moment, Atticus thought the crack had saved the Inspector. Zenia couldn't get the forklift trolley past it to the big front doors.

Then something unexpected happened. The crack began to widen. All the way along the one hundred and fifty-two metres of the great Turbine Hall, the zigzag expanded until it was about twice as wide as it had been before. Atticus watched it in confusion. It looked like Zenia Klob was even more stuck now! But Atticus didn't believe that. Zenia must have some trick hidden up her apron, or his name wasn't Atticus Grammaticus Cattypuss Claw.

'What's that?' Callie pointed in astonishment.

A large metal arm, like a crane, rose up of out the crack. Attached to the end of it was a giant pincer. Zenia stood beside the trolley with a remote control, pushing buttons. The pincer grabbed the camp bed. Then it rotated it until it was vertical and gradually began to lower it into the crack.

'They're going to escape down the crack!' Michael gasped. 'It must lead underground to their getaway vehicle.'

Atticus tried to think what to do. The bed had all but vanished.

'Come on, Biscuit.' Zenia pocketed the remote.

Ginger Biscuit's head and shoulders emerged from the tea urn. He leapt out.

'Let's go,' Zenia said.

The two villains disappeared into the crack after the bed. The crack started to close.

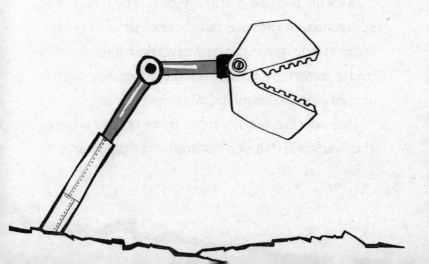

Just then Atticus heard footsteps behind him. It was Zeberdee. He was holding the wafer wrapper in one hand and the hairpin in the other. He stopped when he saw Atticus and the children. Then he stared at the crack in the Turbine Hall in amazement as the zigzag sides inched towards each other.

'What's going on?' he asked in bewilderment.

'They've taken *The Camp Bed*!' Callie told him.

'Dad was lying on it!' Michael said. 'You've got to do something, Zeberdee.'

'Meow!' Atticus pawed at Zeberdee's trouser leg. They had to catch the villains before they bednapped Inspector Cheddar! He raced off.

'Kids, go and get Agent Whelk and your mum.' Zeberdee ran after Atticus along the jagged line to the spot where the bed had disappeared.

Atticus pointed with his tail. The crack had returned to its normal size, but to Atticus's horror, it didn't stop moving. The gap was getting narrower and narrower – if they didn't hurry the villains would close it completely!

'Meow!' He put his front paws on the edge of the crack and dangled his body over the hole.

'Wait for me!' Zeberdee followed suit, wriggling into the tiny space. There was barely any room between Zeberdee's thin frame and the sides of the crack. If they didn't act now, Zeberdee would be crushed. Atticus closed his eyes and let go. He felt Zeberdee do the same.

The two of them dropped together.

SPLASH!

Being a cat, Atticus landed on his feet. He felt water on his paws. He opened his eyes. Zeberdee was beside him, picking himself up. Not being a cat, Zeberdee had landed on his bottom. He was wet through.

Atticus glanced around. They were in a large brick tunnel lit by a soft red glow. VROOM! Atticus heard the roar of an engine. He looked up. The red glow was coming from the tail lights of the villains' getaway vehicle. Atticus could just make it out: a squat bowl-shaped transporter was zooming away from them like a rocket. They were escaping! He splashed down the tunnel after it, gritting his teeth. The claggy water oozed between his toes like paint.

Zeberdee chased after him. The two of them splashed along the tunnel behind the red lights.

VROOM! The vehicle shot out of the tunnel.

Atticus wasn't far behind. The tunnel came out on to a narrow shingle beach. He was beside the River Thames. The tide was out. It lapped against the edge of the shingles. Above him, on the riverbank, Tate Modern towered over the surrounding buildings.

Zeberdee was beside him. 'Now what?' He pointed at the getaway vehicle. Zenia was driving it straight into the river. Around the base of the bowl-shaped transporter ballooned a great inflatable skirt. It was turning into a hovercraft!

VROOM! The hovercraft shot east along the river at incredible speed.

There was nothing else Atticus could do except watch it disappear into the distance until it was out of sight.

13

The next day at Toffly Hall Michael and Callie were having lunch with the Tuckers. Mr Tucker had made hake surprise for the children – the surprise being that it was made with salmon, not hake – but no one seemed very hungry, not even Atticus.

Bones was there too. She looked very nice after her visit to the pet spa on the cruise ship. Her black fur was all shiny and soft and her white teeth gleamed. Atticus wasn't so sure about Mr Tucker, though. He'd been to the pet spa with Bones to have his beard-jumper shampooed. It was now so thick and curly that you could hardly see the rest of him. He'd had hair extensions to match as well, and his eyebrows curled. Atticus thought he looked like an Old English sheepdog.

'Whoose wants some pickle?' Mr Tucker handed round a jar of Butteredsconi's Italian Truffle Pickle.

'No thanks,' Callie said.

'It's very good,' Mr Tucker insisted.

'I don't know how you can eat that stuff after what's happened, Herman!' Mrs Tucker said furiously. She held out her hand.

'All right, all right, Edna, keep your hair on,' Mr Tucker grumbled. He spooned some out on his hake surprise and handed the jar to Mrs Tucker. She threw it in the dustbin.

'What are we going to do?' Callie asked, turning over a bit of mashed potato on her plate with her fork. 'We've got to rescue Dad!'

There had been no sign of the villains since their escape from Tate Modern the previous night.

'I don't see why the police can't just go to Fort Sconi and get him back!' Michael said. 'Everyone knows that's where they're holding him prisoner.'

That was a good point, Atticus thought. Why couldn't they?

'The police need a search warrant,' Mrs Tucker sighed. 'And at the moment they don't have enough

116

evidence to link Butteredsconi with your dad's disappearance.'

'What's a search warrant?' Atticus whispered to Bones. He felt a bit embarrassed having to ask. He thought it was the sort of thing a police cat sergeant should probably know. 'I've never had to search anywhere before,' he explained.

'It's an order from the court,' Bones said, 'to allow the police to enter the building.'

'Oh,' said Atticus. He still wasn't sure why they needed one. Inspector Cheddar usually just barged in.

'What I's don't understand is why Klob and Biscuit would even *take* your dad in the first place,' Mr Tucker ruminated.

'We think they made a mistake, Herman,' Mrs Tucker sighed. 'That modern art is very newfangled. They probably thought he was supposed to be in the bed. And they might not have recognised him with his green hair.'

'But they must realise *now*,' Callie said, 'because Mr Butteredsconi will have told them. So why don't they let Dad go?'

That was the part Atticus didn't understand

either. Why keep the Inspector? Why not just dump him somewhere before he woke up? There was something very strange going on. Atticus was sure. It was instinct – that feeling that you had when you just knew something without being told it. The problem was, he couldn't figure out what.

'I don't know,' Mrs Tucker admitted. She started to collect the plates. 'But I don't see that we've got much choice except to wait. We'll just have to catch Klob's mob when they do their next job. They'll lead us to Fort Sconi, don't you worry. Then we can arrest the whole lot of them and rescue your dad.'

'But how *can* we catch them?' Callie wailed. 'We don't know where they're going to strike next.'

'I'm sure the Commissioner will get another tip-off from Interpol soon,' Mrs Tucker said soothingly. 'Now come and help me with these dishes.'

Callie and Michael got down from the table.

Mr Tucker remained seated. Atticus checked to see that Mrs Tucker's back was turned, then he hopped up on the table and had a quick look for fishy morsels in Mr Tucker's extra-bushy beard-jumper.

'When I's out in me boat catchin' fish,' Mr Tucker said thoughtfully, stroking Atticus between the ears, 'I uses bait.'

'What are you talking about, Herman?' Mrs Tucker asked, crashing about with crockery.

'Well, it's like this, Edna . . .' Mr Tucker removed Atticus with some difficulty from his beard-jumper and set him on the floor. Then he got to his foot and started tapping out a rhythm with his wooden leg.

'Mr Tucker's going to sing a sea shanty!' Callie cried in delight.

The children joined in, clapping. Bones did a little jig. Even Atticus found his whiskers twitching to the beat. He liked Mr Tucker's sea shanties, although they could be a bit gruesome.

Mr Tucker cleared his throat and began:

Worms are great, and so is jelly,
Pickle is the best – it's nice and smelly,
Lizards and flies and shrimps and socks,
Stick 'em in the sea and watch 'em fish flock!
Squished-up toad is nice and mucky,
Most of 'em fish they like it yucky,

They swarm round me boat: that's when I hook 'em,
Then I bash 'em hard on the head and cook 'em.

'Very interesting, I'm sure, Herman,' Mrs Tucker said. 'But what's it got to do with rescuing Inspector Cheddar?'

'What I's saying is that villains are like fish,' Mr Tucker explained. 'You need bait to catch 'em.' He lit his pipe. A thick cloud of blue smoke filled the room. Everyone started coughing. 'Only instead of using worrrrms,' Mr Tucker said, 'you use something else!'

'Like what?' Mrs Tucker was nonplussed.

'Aaaarrrrt,' said Mr Tucker. He sucked noisily on his pipe.

Callie gave a whoop of delight. 'That's brilliant, Mr Tucker!'

'But we don't *have* any art.' Mrs Tucker frowned.

'We can get some, though.' Michael grinned at his sister.

Callie grinned back.

'How?' Mrs Tucker still didn't get it.

Atticus wasn't sure if he did either. The sort of art Ricardo Butteredsconi wanted Klob and Biscuit to steal was very expensive. Atticus didn't think they could afford any: you couldn't exactly pay for it with sardines. And Mr and Mrs Tucker had just spent a lot of money on their cruise. He looked at the children, puzzled.

'Atticus can paint it, of course!' Callie laughed. 'Ricardo Butteredsconi loves his pictures! He thinks Atticus is art's NEXT BIG THING. He said so when we visited the pickle factory.'

'Callie's right, Mrs Tucker. If Atticus does more paintings Butteredsconi's bound to want Klob and Biscuit to steal one for his collection,' Michael added. 'It's obvious!'

Of course! Atticus purred with pleasure. What with everything else that had happened recently, he'd forgotten that he was going to be art's NEXT BIG THING. Now he had a chance to do more painting *and* help the Cheddars.

Mrs Tucker punched the air. 'Well done, Herman,' she said. 'That pet spa treatment obviously did you good.' She planted a kiss on his hair extensions. 'You may be as hairy as a catfish, but you do have very good ideas sometimes.' She scooped up Atticus. 'Right,' she said. 'Let's get

121

started. I'll phone your mum and tell her what we're going to do. We'll arrange the exhibition here at Toffly Hall.'

'What shall we call it?' Callie asked. 'It's got to have a name.'

'How about TOTALLY PAWSOME,' Michael suggested.

TOTALLY PAWSOME. Atticus thought he could live with that.

That afternoon, Atticus got to work.

Mrs Cheddar thought the exhibition was a marvellous idea and she asked Zeberdee Cronk along to help as well. Zeberdee said Atticus should use oil paint, which he brought with him in tubes. Oil paint, Atticus quickly discovered, was thick and sticky and smelly and took ages to dry. Luckily, Bones and the children were on hand to wipe Atticus's paws with Thumpers' Traditional Paint Remover to keep them clean.

Zeberdee also brought something called canvas instead of paper for Atticus to paint on. Canvas was a kind of thick material – the sort that cats like to scratch to keep their claws sharp. It was a lot more difficult to cover with paw prints than paper

so Atticus took to walking across it with all four paws drenched in different coloured paint, which he thought was very daring.

Zeberdee and Mrs Cheddar said it looked fantastic.

Then, by mistake, Atticus got his tail in a pot of yellow paint while Michael was cleaning his paws. He swished it to and fro to try and get it off and it went all over another canvas that he'd sat on accidentally and Zeberdee said that was good too – they should call it *The Beach at Littleton-on-Sea*, which is what they did. Atticus finished it off with a few blue splodges for the sea and a couple of brown ones for the beach huts where he usually met Mimi.

With Zeberdee's help, he even managed to hold

a pencil in his paw and draw a few wobbly lines which was supposed to be a picture of him with the children. It wasn't quite Picasso, but everyone said it was pretty amazing for a cat to be able to draw at all, so that went into the exhibition too.

Then Zeberdee took some photos and wrote something on the computer which he said was going to be published in an art magazine so that the villains would know all about the exhibition.

'That's right, me boy, luuuurrrrre them in!' Mr Tucker agreed.

Mrs Tucker fed Atticus on fresh sardines to keep his strength up and Mr Tucker went out on his boat to fish for them. That night, instead of going back to number 2 Blossom Crescent with Callie and Michael, Atticus stayed at Toffly Hall with Bones so that he could paint more pictures in the morning. Bones, who was a very tidy cat, made his basket and plumped up the cushions on the sofa so he could lie on them if he preferred. She massaged his paws with the Thumpers' Traditional Paw Cream that she'd got at the pet spa to stop his pads getting dried out.

The next day, when everything was finally ready Mimi came to see him with her owner Aysha and Aysha's baby. Zeberdee was hanging the last of the paintings on the wall. When the baby saw all the lovely colours she laughed and pointed with pleasure.

'This is as colourful as my flower shop!' Aysha said. 'Well done, Atticus! Can you paint one for me?'

Atticus purred to show that he would be happy to.

'I'm so proud of you, Atticus!' Mimi said.

'Do you like them?' Atticus asked. It was ages since he'd seen Mimi and being around her always made him feel a bit shy.

'Of course I do!'

'Really?'

'Really!' Mimi twined her tail around his.

Atticus was pleased. But despite the fact that Mimi was there and everyone was spoiling him, for some reason Atticus didn't feel very happy.

'What's up?' Mimi asked. She always had an uncanny knack of knowing when something was wrong.

'It's Inspector Cheddar,' Atticus said. 'The kids don't understand why Ricardo Butteredsconi is keeping him prisoner and neither do I.'

'Maybe it's because he's worried Inspector Cheddar will lead the police to the stolen art,' Mimi suggested.

'I suppose so . . .' Atticus said. 'I don't think it's that, though. They could have let him go at the beginning, when they realised their mistake.' He shook his head. 'I have this awful feeling that Butteredsconi is keeping him for a different reason . . .' He paused. 'Something to do with art.'

'Art?' Mimi repeated. 'But Inspector Cheddar doesn't know anything about art.'

'That's why it's so weird,' Atticus said. 'And Butteredsconi – he's weird too. He's obsessed with pickled animals. The whole set-up is creepy.' He told Mimi about the history of Sconi Point and the crazy ride in the tunnel under the sea.

Mimi shivered when she heard the part about the mad doctor doing experiments on his patients.

'He sounds like Frankenstein,' she said.

'That's exactly what Michael said,' Atticus remarked. He sighed. 'This art business, Mimi, I don't really understand it. I mean, why is a pickled animal or a camp bed art? I thought I was getting the hang of it with Zeberdee but I'm not so sure now. Why would someone pay a fortune for a picture of a person in mixed-up squares like a Rubik's cube? Or a cat's paw prints?' He sighed. 'Maybe if I understood that, I could work out what the villains want with Inspector Cheddar.'

'What do you think art is, Atticus?' Mimi asked him.

Atticus groomed his whiskers. 'I was hoping you were going to tell me that,' he said cheekily.

'No, I'm being serious,' Mimi replied. 'What do you think it is?'

'Well,' Atticus considered the question. 'At first I thought it was paintings or statues. Then I realised that it could be all sorts of things, like pickled animals, or beds. Then Callie and Michael explained art doesn't have to look like what it actually is – like Picasso, for instance. And then Zeberdee said it could have a meaning, like *Plastic*

Ocean. And *then* I found out it could be interesting to look at, like the crack . . . Or fun to do, like my paw prints.'

'Go on . . .' Mimi encouraged him.

'So I guess Michael and Callie were right: art is something that makes you see things a bit differently,' he offered.

'That's brilliant!' Mimi said. 'I couldn't have explained it better myself.' She looked at him. 'Does that help?'

Atticus shook his head. 'No.' He managed a brief purr. 'But thanks anyway.' He squeezed Mimi's paw. 'I'm sure I'll work it out.'

'There!' Zeberdee finished hanging the last picture.

'I think we're ready.' Mrs Tucker came bustling up with the children. She looked around the exhibition and nodded. 'Good work, everyone,' she said.

'Mrs Tucker has bugged all the paintings with tracking devices in case the villains give us the slip again,' Michael told Atticus.

'So we can trace them to Fort Sconi,' Callie explained, 'and rescue Dad.'

That was a good idea, Atticus thought. He glanced at Mimi. He just hoped they wouldn't be too late.

Mrs Tucker gave the two cats a sardine to share. 'Now all we've got to do is sit back and wait for them to take the bait.'

15

'Totally Pawsome!' Ginger Biscuit spat the words
out as if they were a rat's stomach. 'Atticus Claw?!
An artist?! That cat makes me want to puke.'

He and the magpies were hiding in Zenia Klob's
squeaky wheelie bin outside the gates of Toffly
Hall. Zenia was disguised as a rubbish collector.
They had been sent by Ricardo Butteredsconi to
steal Atticus's new paintings. There was one in
particular he wanted; the one entitled *The Beach at
Littleton-on-Sea*.

'Oh, I don't know, Ginge . . .' Slasher began. He
was reading the latest edition of a glossy magazine
called *Art for the Filthy Rich*. There was a photo of
Atticus on the front cover, under the caption 'Cat
Art is the New Cool'. 'Some of his stuff's not bad.'

'I didn't know he could draw,' Thug said conversationally.

'He can't.' Biscuit snarled.

Thug and Slasher traded looks. Thug winked at Slasher. Now was their chance to wind Biscuit up!

'You sure about that, Ginge?' Slasher said slowly, turning the pages and pretending to look at them carefully. 'Says here he's pretty good at it. What d'you reckon, Thug?'

'Oh, yes, Slasher, my friend,' Thug said importantly. 'He's totally pawsome, in my 'umble hop-inion.'

'Totally awful, you mean,' Ginger Biscuit growled.

'Ah, come on, Ginge,' Slasher nudged Thug. 'Credit where credit's due: you've got to admit it's probably better than what you could do, at any rate.'

'I doubt it,' Ginger Biscuit retorted. 'I just haven't tried, that's all.'

'Sounds like sour grapes to me,' Thug commented. ''Ere, Slash,' he said, leaning over Slasher's shoulder to look at the magazine, 'that painting of Littleton-on-Sea what we've come to pinch ... says here it's worth two million smackers.'

'Grrrr ...' Ginger Biscuit snarled.

'Maybe you and Zenia should think of investing in one with all that money Butteredsconi's paying you?' Slasher suggested. 'An original Claw. Nice thing to show your grandkids.'

'Definitely,' Thug agreed. 'Look lovely in Gulag Cottage, that would. Every time you look at it you can think about how much dosh Claw's raking in. And how famous he is.'

'Shut up!' Ginger Biscuit growled, pinning each magpie with a front paw. 'He'll be dead by then anyway.' He dangled them upside down. 'And if either of you dare tell me what a brilliant artist Atticus Claw is ever again, so will you.' His pale eyes gleamed. 'How about I have you stuffed and hung over the fireplace at Gulag Cottage instead so every time I look at *you* I can think about how much fun it was ripping your heads off with my teeth.'

'Chaka-chaka-chaka-chaka-chaka!' Thug and Slasher struggled and flapped.

'Let them go,' Jimmy Magpie said. 'We've got a job to do.'

Squeak . . . squeak . . . squeak . . . squeak.

The wheelie bin was on the move.

Crunch. Crunch. Crunch. Crunch.

Zenia's boots crunched on the gravel as she pushed it up the drive.

'Remember the drill,' Biscuit said, releasing the magpies reluctantly.

Jimmy nodded. '*We'll* remember the drill if *you* remember your promise,' he said. 'I want Claw flat once this is over. No excuses. Vroom. Squish, squash. Like the humans did to our magpie mates. Then you feed Pam to Pork and let us go. All right?'

'All right,' Ginger Biscuit grumbled.

The bin came to a halt. The lid opened. Zenia's ugly mug peered in. 'Off you go, birdies,' she said. 'Time to peck the vires.'

The magpies flew off.

'Okay, Biscuit,' Zenia said. 'Atticus's exhibition is in the ballroom. The painting Mr Butteredsconi vants is by the French doors: you know the vun.'

'Grrrr . . .' Yes, Ginger Biscuit knew the one. He'd had it rammed down his throat enough times by

134

Butteredsconi after the mistake they'd made with the camp bed, although – surprisingly – Butteredsconi hadn't been as cross about finding the bloke with green hair in it as Ginger Biscuit expected he would be. In fact, Butteredsconi and Zenia had a good old laugh about it afterwards. Ginger Biscuit didn't know what they'd done with him; the bed was hidden somewhere at Fort Sconi with all the other stuff they'd snatched. And he didn't care. What he wanted was revenge on Atticus – and sooner rather than later. The idea that Atticus was art's NEXT BIG THING made him seethe with spite.

Ginger Biscuit disappeared into the shrubbery. He wriggled his way through the bushes until he reached the French doors that led from the ballroom into the garden. He felt like smashing them with a brick instead of waiting for the magpies to disable the alarm and pick the lock with his claws. Actually, why the heck not? With any luck he'd ruin Atticus's rotten painting in the process. He picked up the nearest rock.

'Not so fast, my vindow-smashing mewster.' Zenia squeezed in beside him. She plucked the

135

rock from his paw. 'Remember, Biscuit,' she crooned, 'revenge is sveeter ven served up pickled.'

'Myaw?' Ginger Biscuit was puzzled.

'Be patient, my foul-tempered furry fury,' Zenia said. 'You vill have your revenge on Atticus. Mr Butteredsconi is a vicked villain, like us, don't forget.' She fed him a pickled rat's tail from her coat sleeve. 'Atticus's paintings may be vorth a fortune, Biscuit, but you and I know this is a trick. Atticus and Agent Velk vant to find the stolen vorks of art. And Inspector Cheddar, of course . . .'

Inspector Cheddar? Ginger Biscuit nearly choked on his pickled rat's tail. Surely she didn't mean . . .

'Yes, Biscuit, it vos Atticus's bungling boss ve bednapped by mistake!' she cackled. 'Vot a laugh, eh?'

'Myaw?' Ginger Biscuit moaned. He hoped Zenia knew what she was doing. Stealing art was one thing. Bednapping a member of the fuzz was another. He didn't want to spend the rest of his life behind bars.

'Don't vorry, my precious predator,' Zenia reassured him. 'Ve are vun step ahead of Velk. Ve vill keep the Inspector under vraps until the heat's off. He hasn't got a clue vot's going on; I've given him a dose of my super-strong sleeping potion. And Velk and Atticus can't act vithout proof.' She scratched Biscuit's ears. 'Besides, Ricardo has very special plans for him.' She leaned down and whispered something to Biscuit.

Ginger Biscuit's pale blue eyes registered astonishment, then understanding, and finally cunning. A deep, satisfied purr reverberated across his body.

Zenia was right.

Revenge was best served up pickled.

16

Beep! Beep! Beep!

Outside the gates of Butteredsconi's Pickle Factory, Atticus was on watch with Callie and Michael. The three of them were holed up in a police surveillance vehicle with Mrs Tucker and Mrs Cheddar. The surveillance vehicle was disguised as a cabbage delivery lorry. So far the disguise seemed to be working: none of the workers had come out of the factory to ask any questions.

Beep! Beep! Beep!

'It's coming from the fort,' Mrs Tucker said. The beeping was being transmitted from the tracking device on the back of Atticus's stolen painting to a computer in the lorry. The screen flashed with a little green dot. 'It's on the second floor. About five metres behind the window.' The computer tracking system was very sophisticated: it could pinpoint the exact location of the bug.

She shifted the lorry into gear and drove a little way along the coast to where the road petered out.

Atticus peeked through the window of the lorry. Fort Sconi was directly opposite. It loomed out of the sea, solid and forbidding. There weren't many windows. Atticus supposed it was to stop the invaders from getting in back in the olden days. It stopped anyone getting out as well, including Inspector Cheddar, he thought gloomily. The only window Atticus could see was a narrow slit about halfway up the building. It was clad in iron bars.

Beep! Beep! Beep!

'Atticus's painting is definitely in there,' Mrs Tucker said. She picked up her mobile phone. 'I'll phone the Commissioner for a search warrant. Then we'll find the painting and arrest the lot of them.'

The warrant came through within minutes. Mrs Tucker printed it off and tucked it into her bra.

'Let's go and find Herman,' she said.

Callie and Michael jumped out of the lorry with Atticus, closely followed by Mrs Tucker and Mrs Cheddar. They scrambled down the bank to the sea. At the bottom of the bank was a jetty. Moored up beside it was a fishing boat with writing on the side: *The Jolly Jellyfish*.

The Jolly Jellyfish was the name of Mr Tucker's boat. Mr Tucker popped his head out of the cabin. 'Come on, youze lot. Me and Bones is ready for action.'

They jumped on board. Mr Tucker handed round life jackets for everyone – there was even a cat-sized one for Atticus – then he started the engine.

Zoom! The Jolly Jellyfish zipped away from the jetty towards the fort. 'Here, kids, take the wheel,' Mr Tucker said. 'Me and Bones will go and put another bottle of shaaarrrrk faaarrrt in the tank.' Shark fart was Mr Tucker's favourite fuel. It made the boat go very fast.

Callie and Michael took turns to steer while Mrs Cheddar checked with the binoculars to make sure they weren't being watched. Mrs Tucker handed round fish-paste sandwiches she'd brought with

her in her basket. Atticus chewed his gratefully –
sailing was hungry work even if you weren't doing
anything.

The closer they got to the fort, the scarier it
looked. The walls were grey and splattered with
bird poo. Sharp rocks poked out of the sea around
the base. The sea was choppy and white.

'The landing point is on the other side,' Mr
Tucker said, returning with Bones. 'We's need to
get into the channel. Or we'll run aground.' He
took the wheel. *The Jolly Jellyfish* rounded the rocks.
The little fishing boat pitched and rolled: the
current was surprisingly strong. Atticus felt sick.

'Look at the horizon, Atticus,' Bones reminded
him.

Atticus looked grimly out to sea.

Gradually the water became calmer as the boat
entered the channel.

Putt. Putt. Putt. Putt. Putt.

Mr Tucker eased *The Jolly Jellyfish* into land.

The landing point was big enough for several
large boats. A crane
towered above it for
lifting supplies.

But it was empty apart from *The Jolly Jellyfish*. Atticus looked round. There was no sign of the villain's getaway vessel he and Zeberdee had chased along the banks of the Thames: Klob must have hidden it somewhere.

Bones leapt out and tied the fishing boat to the moorings with a rope. The little group made their way up wide slippery steps to the front door of Fort Sconi.

The first thing that Atticus saw was a sign that said:

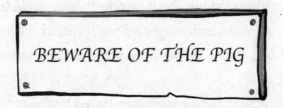

BEWARE OF THE PIG

'Remember what happened to Dad,' Mrs Cheddar warned the kids. 'Whatever you do, don't get on the wrong side of that horrible pig. We don't want anyone else ending up in the pickling tank.'

They had laughed about it at the time, Atticus remembered, in the car going back from Butteredsconi's pickle factory. It didn't seem very funny now. Everyone's face was deadly serious.

BASH! BASH! BASH!

'Open up!' Mrs Tucker shouted.

The door opened with a slight creak. An old woman in a maid's uniform peered through the gap. 'Can I help you?' she asked.

'We have a warrant to search the premises,' Mrs Tucker waved it in the maid's face. 'Stand aside.'

'But Mr Butteredsconi vasn't expecting anyone . . .'

'Too bad!'

The maid looked on as they pushed their way in.

'Where is he?' Mrs Tucker demanded.

'Upstairs, in the drawing room,' the maid said.

Atticus followed Mrs Tucker up the elegant staircase. To Atticus's surprise, the interior of Fort Sconi was absolutely gorgeous; if he hadn't been on a police inquiry he would have stopped to admire all the wonderful decorations and paintings that hung from the walls. He could see why Ginger Biscuit and Zenia would want to work for Ricardo Butteredsconi: the pickle giant was obviously loaded.

Beep! BEEP! BEEP!

'This is it,' Mrs Tucker puffed as they reached the second floor drawing room. Mr Tucker limped up the stairs behind, cursing his wooden leg.

Mrs Tucker kicked the door open. They entered the room.

Ricardo Butteredsconi rolled off an exquisite silk sofa to greet them. So did Pork. Atticus's eyes moved from one to the other. It was *extraordinary* how similar they looked, he thought.

'Which one's the pig?' Mr Tucker whispered.

'My guess is the one wearing the suit and tie is Butteredsconi,' Mrs Tucker hissed, 'and the one with parrot droppings on his head and strings of spaghetti dripping from his snout is Pork. Am I right, kids?'

Callie and Michael nodded.

Ricardo Butteredsconi gave a little bow. His chins wobbled. 'What a lovely surprise,' he said. 'Do come in.'

17

'To what do I owe the pleasure ... Ms ... er?' Butteredsconi extended a meaty mitt to Mrs Tucker.

'It's Agent, not Ms,' Mrs Tucker snapped. 'Agent Whelk, MI6. This is my husband, Herman. You've already met the Cheddars.'

Butteredsconi's piggy eyes fell on Mrs Cheddar, Callie and Michael. Then he saw Atticus. 'Ah.' Ricardo Butteredsconi smiled. 'The worthy winner of our pickle-painting competition. I've been reading all about you. He pointed to a low table. A copy of *Art for the Filthy Rich* sat upon it. 'I knew you were destined for greatness. I particularly liked your painting of the beach at Littleton-on-Sea.'

You didn't just like it, Atticus thought. *You nicked it.*

'What have you done with Dad?' Callie shouted.

'Dad?' Ricardo Butteredsconi repeated. 'You mean the Inspector who fell in the cabbage vat?' He sighed. 'I'm afraid he had very little appreciation of either art or pickle.'

'He didn't *fall* in the cabbage vat,' Mrs Cheddar said stiffly, holding Michael and Callie's hands. 'Your pig pushed him deliberately.'

Pork grunted. He seemed pleased with himself.

'Where is Dad?' Michael shouted.

'I have no idea what you're talking about,' Ricardo Butteredsconi replied coldly. 'Do you, Pork?'

Pork shook his head. Slobber sprayed from his lips.

'Don't pretend you don't know,' Mrs Tucker fumed. 'Inspector Cheddar was in the camp bed you had Klob and Biscuit steal from Tate Modern.'

'Klob and Biscuit?' Ricardo Butteredsconi turned to Pork. 'I fear the dear lady is mad,' he said, 'like the poor doctor who used to live here.'

Pork snorted his agreement.

Atticus tensed. Calling Mrs Tucker mad was never going to be a good idea.

'Look, fatso,' Mrs Tucker rolled up her sleeves.

'I've had just about enough of this.' Atticus was interested to see that Mrs Tucker had a new tattoo on her forearm. She must have had it done at the pet spa. It said:

DON'T MESS WITH EDNA IF YOU WANT TO KEEP YOUR TEETH

It was probably good advice, he thought.

'*You* are the criminal mastermind behind the recent international art thefts,' she accused Butteredsconi. 'Don't deny it.'

'Me? Steal art?' Butteredsconi gasped. 'But Agent Whelk, I love art: ask Atticus and these delightful children and their dear mother.' He clasped his hands together. 'I told them of my passion when they visited my factory. I would never, ever, EVER do anything like that.' Tears rolled down his pillowy cheeks. 'I am deeply wounded that you would think such a thing.'

He was a good actor, Atticus had to admit. But the fact that Pork's head was covered in Pam's parrot poop was a dead giveaway. And there were other clues to show that the villains had been here. Half a pickled rat's tail lay on the table; there was ginger fur on the shagpile carpet; the pickled fruit in the fruit bowl had been pecked; and beside a gleaming gold bucket and a pile of straw lay a few magpie feathers and a packet of Thumpers' Scrubbit. Biscuit had been here; so had the magpies and Pam. And all the signs indicated that they had left in a hurry. They were probably hiding somewhere in the fort.

'Spare us the waterworks, Butteredsconi,' Mrs Tucker barked. 'We know you're in on the art crime. We know you found Klob and her gang in the megalodon. We know you're paying them a lot of money to steal art for you. We know they bednapped Inspector Cheddar by mistake.'

Ricardo Butteredsconi blew his nose on a large silk handkerchief. He drew himself up so that he was almost as tall as he was wide. 'Agent Whelk, you come into my home and make these terrible accusations against me.' His expression changed to one of cunning. 'But let me ask *you* a question: where is your proof?'

Mrs Tucker waved a gadget at him. 'This is a

tracking device,' she said. 'We placed a bug on the back of one of the paintings you ordered Klob to steal – the beach scene by Atticus. The tracking device has traced the picture to this room. The painting is here, in *your* fort. That's our proof. Now get out of the way while we search for it.'

Atticus couldn't help admiring Mrs Tucker. She didn't seem at all fazed by Ricardo Butteredsconi. Atticus was, though. The pickle giant gave him the creeps. It wasn't just the way the single strand of greasy hair oiled its way between his ears like a squashed slug, or even the way his nostril hair quivered like a batch of mould under a microscope: it was the fact that Ricardo Butteredsconi didn't seem to care at all about the kids or Mrs Cheddar. He didn't care that he was accused of being an international criminal mastermind. Worst of all, he didn't care that he was holding Inspector Cheddar prisoner against his will.

Ricardo Butteredsconi wasn't just weird, Atticus decided, he was downright dangerous.

Mrs Tucker advanced with the tracking device.

Beep! Beep! Beep! BEEEEEEEEEEEP!!

'It's in there.' Mrs Tucker pointed at the pile of straw. 'Search it, Herman!'

Mr Tucker hobbled forward. He dug into the straw with his hands.

'There's nothing here,' Mr Tucker said.

'It's in there somewhere, Herman,' Mrs Tucker said firmly. 'Keep looking.'

'All right, all right!' Mr Tucker fumbled about. 'Wait! I's found something!' He frowned. 'But it ain't a painting.' He withdrew his hands. They were covered in pig slurry. Mr Tucker sniffed it. 'That smells even stronger than shaarrrkk faaarrrrt,' he said. 'Mind if I take some with me to try in me engine?' he asked Pork.

Pork grunted.

'Thanks.' Mr Tucker produced a container from somewhere in his trousers and started shovelling pig poop into it.

'It seems that your tracker device must be faulty, Agent Whelk,' Butteredsconi said lightly. 'If I *had* stolen something as valuable as an Atticus Claw painting, I would hardly be likely to hide it in Pork's lavatory, would I? Now, kindly leave, or I will telephone your superior and have *you* arrested for invading my home.' Ricardo Butteredsconi had stopped crying. His face was stony and his voice cold.

Mrs Tucker was momentarily speechless.

Atticus decided to give it one last try. He approached Pork. 'You ate the bug, Pork,' he hissed, 'so where's the painting? And what have you done with Inspector Cheddar?'

Pork looked at him blearily. 'Not telling,' he grunted.

Mrs Tucker put her hands on her hips and faced the pickle giant. 'I know you've got Atticus's painting,' she hissed, 'and the rest of the stolen art; and Inspector Cheddar, for that matter. And you can bet your barnacles we'll find them. And when we do,' she shook her fist at him, 'it will give me great pleasure to throw you and your pestilent pig in jail and put you both on a diet of bread and water.'

The maid let them out. 'Goodbye,' she said. 'Don't come again, vill you?'

The dejected group boarded *The Jolly Jellyfish*. Mr Tucker dropped Mrs Tucker off at the jetty to collect the lorry. Then they puttered back along the coast in silence to Littleton-on-Sea.

It was only when Atticus got back to number 2 Blossom Crescent with Mrs Cheddar and the kids that he realised they had been tricked again: the maid was none other than Zenia Klob in one of her many disguises.

Mimi came by after supper. She had been allowed to stay the night while Aysha took her baby to see her grandparents.

'There's nothing more you can do tonight, Atticus,' she said, touching his paw. 'Let's get some sleep.'

The two cats padded upstairs to the children's bedroom. Atticus curled up on the end of Michael's bed and Mimi on the end of Callie's.

'We will find him, won't we, Michael?' Callie sniffed.

'Of course we will,' Michael replied fiercely.

The two children went to sleep.

Atticus felt restless. His instinct told him that Inspector Cheddar was in terrible danger. But

Mimi was right. There was nothing more they could do that night. They would have to wait for the morning and see if Mrs Tucker could get another search warrant.

In the middle of the night, Atticus woke clutching his chewed ear. He had been dreaming about the ride at Butteredsconi's pickle factory. In his dream, the ride didn't end. He couldn't get off the cart. He had to go round and round again. Each time his eyes stung more from the horrible smell of vinegar and spices, and his fur became more salty and matted until he could hardly move, so that eventually, when the giant teeth chomped down on the burger, they chomped down on him instead. Then the scene changed to the drawing room at Fort Sconi and it wasn't a pair of giant plastic teeth chomping at him any more, it was a set of gleaming feline ones that belonged to Ginger Biscuit . . .

'Are you all right?' Mimi whispered.

'Not really,' Atticus admitted. 'I was having a bad dream.' He stretched. 'I might go and get a drink of water.' His mouth felt dry – as if he'd swallowed salt.

'I'll join you,' Mimi purred.

Silently the two cats got off the end of children's beds and padded into the kitchen.

Atticus lapped thirstily at his bowl of water. Then he sat back and wiped his whiskers. 'That's the second awful dream I've had recently,' he mentioned.

'What was the first one?' Mimi asked.

Atticus shuddered. 'I don't want to think about it,' he said.

'Sometimes your dreams tell you things, Atticus,' Mimi said gently. 'Things that you can't see when you're awake.'

'You mean it might be important?'

'It might be,' Mimi purred.

'Well . . .' Atticus thought back. 'It was when I was in the limo coming back from the visit to the pickle factory,' he recalled. 'Butteredsconi had spent ages telling us about his pickled art collection and it freaked me out. I was trying to go to sleep but I couldn't because all I could see in my head were huge jars full of pickled animals.'

'Go on,' Mimi prompted.

'And then I must have dozed off,' Atticus said, 'because I had this awful nightmare that Inspector Cheddar was one of the animals in the pickle jars . . .' He stopped abruptly. Suddenly he understood.

'What is it, Atticus?' Mimi asked.

'I know why Butteredsconi is keeping Inspector Cheddar,' Atticus gasped. He held his face in his paws. 'How could I have been so blind?'

'What do you mean?'

'The kids were joking in the car about Inspector Cheddar falling in the pickle tank,' Atticus moaned. 'Michael said something about him being like one of Butteredsconi's pickled animals and then . . .' He could hardly get the words out. 'Callie said he might end up as part of Butteredsconi's art collection.'

Mimi's eyes were wide with horror. 'No . . .'

Atticus gripped her paw. 'That's got to be it, Mimi. That's the reason Butteredsconi is keeping Inspector Cheddar prisoner. He's going to pickle him and add him to his art collection. It's the *reverse* of Frankenstein! Instead of turning a corpse into a living human, he's turning a living human into a corpse . . .'

Atticus started towards the cat flap. 'We've got to get back to Fort Sconi before it's too late!'

'But how can we?'

Just then the doorbell rang.

'Who's that?' Atticus wondered aloud. He hoped it wasn't more bad news.

The two cats went into the hall.

'Coming!' Mrs Cheddar hurried downstairs in her dressing gown and opened the front door.

'Mrs Tucker!' she exclaimed.

Mrs Tucker was wearing her biker boots and helmet. Her face was set in a determined expression. 'Get the kids,' she said. 'And the cats.'

'But where are we going?'

'Back to Sconi Point,' Mrs Tucker said. 'I want to have another look around that fort.'

'But don't we need another warrant?' Mrs Cheddar said.

Mrs Tucker slammed on her helmet. 'Not if we go in through the tunnel,' she said.

Deep in the basement of Fort Sconi, Thug and Slasher were busy polishing a large metal table with two rags and a tin of Thumpers' Traditional Slab Brite.

The surface of the table gleamed and twinkled in the bright electric light that flooded the white-tiled room. You might have thought this would please the magpies because normally, as you will recall, they loved shiny things. However, on this occasion it didn't please them at all. This was partly because the metal table was too big to steal. However it was mainly on account of what the table was going to be used for.

'I don't like this,' Thug said nervously.

'Me neither,' Slasher agreed. He pulled a face. 'I

never thought I'd hear myself say this, Thug, me old mate, but I'd rather clean Pam's poo bucket.'

'I'd rather scrub Pork's bum,' Thug said gloomily. 'This place gives me the creeps.'

The two birds were in Ricardo Butteredsconi's private pickling laboratory.

This was where he and Pork spent the three hundred and sixty-four days of the year that they weren't in the pickle factory. It was where they preserved bats, rats, gnats, lizards, monkeys, mice, lice, spiders, snakes, drakes, goats, stoats, moles, voles, scorpions, millipedes, zillipedes, trillipedes, hogs, frogs, loads of toads, quails, snails, baby whales, sows, cows, bugs, pugs, slugs, weevils, beavers, chicks, ticks, foxes, oxes, germs, worms, bees, fleas and manatees . . . and, of course, sharks, and stuck them into jars and tanks.

It was where they had pickled the megalodon.

It was where they planned to pickle Inspector Cheddar later that night.

'This is where the patients from the old hospital were brought when they *died*,' Slasher hissed.

'Don't remind me!' Thug looked pale. Zenia had told them all about the mad doctor and his experiments the day before.

'Yeah, but you fainted before Zenia got to the really gruesome bit,' Slasher insisted.

'Go on, then,' Thug said, his curiosity getting the better of him.

'This is the mortuary slab,' Slasher went on, 'what he laid the corpses on whilst he got them ready.'

'What do you mean, got them ready?' Thug asked.

'Well, you know, pickled them like what Butteredsconi does with his vegetables and animals and stuff so they didn't smell too much whilst he was experimenting on them.'

'Maybe we should have tried that with Beaky,' Thug said thoughtfully. Beaky was one of their friends who had been killed by a passing car. The magpies had held a funeral for him. 'He'd got a bit whiffy by the time we had our gathering.'

'Yeah, maybe,' Slasher agreed.

The two magpies stopped for a rest.

'You missed a bit!' Pam the parrot was in charge of the cleaning operation.

Pam wasn't at all squeamish. Nor was Pork. The

idea of pickling a human made them guffaw with laughter, particularly when Zenia told them they would both get to help.

Pam took off from her perch and landed on the table. She pointed at a rusty coloured spot of gunk with her wing. 'Clean it up!' she squawked at Thug.

'I can't,' Thug moaned. 'Not after what Slasher just told me. I'll be sick.'

'Pass the Slab Brite, Thug,' Slasher sighed. 'I'll do it.'

Thug pushed the jar towards his friend with his toe, averting his eyes from the label.

THUMPERS'
Traditional Slab Brite
For all your mortuary needs

Removes even the toughest bloodstains

Not to mention all the other yucky bits
like brains!

Slasher dipped his rag into the polish and rubbed away at the rusty spot.

'Good.' Pam pronounced herself satisfied. 'Now go and help Jim with the embalming tank.'

Jimmy Magpie was performing a similar task on a large copper cylinder next to the mortuary table. The cylinder had tubes sticking out of it and a pedal at the bottom attached to a pump.

'No way!' Thug objected. 'It's too gruesome. It's like something out of a horror film. You know, one of them ones where zombies pop up and pull all your feathers out.'

'Gruesome, poosome!' Pam nipped at him. 'Go and help or I'll tell Pork I want to pickle YOU!'

'Okay, okay!' Thug shuffled off the table with his rag in his beak. He dropped to the tiled floor in a flutter of feathers, grumbling to himself. 'Chaka-chaka-chaka-chaka-chaka!'

Slasher flew after him. They joined their boss at the base of the embalming tank.

'Get on with it, Jim!' Pam snapped. 'You've still got the surgical instruments and the drainage vat to go.'

'Shut up, you old bat,' Jimmy shouted back.

'Can't you see I'm doing it?' Jimmy had nearly finished the tank. Beside the cylinder was a large copper basin. Next to that was a tray full of hypodermic needles, syringes, scalpels and various pairs of curiously shaped scissors.

'She's not going to make us watch, is she?' Thug said in a pathetic voice, eyeing the equipment.

Jimmy shrugged. 'I don't know. I wish they'd pickle her instead. Anyway,' he added, 'I don't see why you're so uptight about it, Thug. We hate humans, remember? They're car-driving magpie mashers. It's them that turned Beaky into roadkill. They don't think anything about mangling *us*. This is our chance to get even.'

'You've got to admit the boss is right, Thug,' Slasher agreed. 'It was Inspector Cheese who put us in the slammer in the first place. He deserves it.' He put a comforting wing around Thug. 'Don't worry, it won't be that bad. All they're going to do is drain his blood out and inject him with formaldehyde.'

'Form-al-de-doody what?' Thug asked weakly.

'It's a posh name for pickle juice,' Slasher explained. 'Anyway, then they're going to pop him in a pickling tank like the megalodon so that Butteredsconi and Pork can look at him floating about. I mean, where's the harm in that?' He gave Thug a little squeeze. 'And it's not like he'll feel anything cos he's asleep. Although,' he added as an afterthought, 'it could get a bit messy when the pump starts.'

PLOOMPH! Thug slipped from under Slasher's wing and passed out on the tiles.

Just then Ginger Biscuit sauntered in. 'Not long now, boys!' He cast a meaningful glance at Pam. The intention was that Biscuit would make Pam 'disappear' after Inspector Cheddar was pickled. Then they would be freed.

'What about Claw?' Jimmy demanded.

'Don't worry about him,' Ginger Biscuit said. 'There's nothing more he and the rest of those sickening do-gooders can do without another search warrant. By the time they get here – *if* they get here – Inspector Cheddar will be Butteredsconi's prize exhibit, Pam will be in Pork's stomach and we'll be long gone. Then we'll bide our time, go back to Littleton-on-Sea when Claw's not expecting us and squish him, just like we planned. Vroom, squish, squash. Okay?'

'What if he comes anyway,' Jimmy insisted, 'without the others?'

Ginger Biscuit grinned. 'I hope he does,' he said. 'There's plenty of room in the pickling tank for him as well. Besides,' he added, 'the security at this place is crazy . . .' He paused meaningfully. 'And I *mean* crazy.'

He bent down and whispered something to Jimmy.

Jimmy's eyes gleamed. 'Nice,' he said, 'very nice. I couldn't have thought of anything more devious myself.' He drew himself up and stretched his wings, examining the glossy blue sheen on the tips. Then he spread his tail feathers and did the same with the green shine on those. He looked twice the size he had a moment ago and a whole lot more evil.

Thug had woken up. He and Slasher watched Jimmy Magpie with a growing sense of excitement. To tell the truth, they'd been a bit worried about how parrot-pecked their boss had become since his marriage to Pam. But this looked more like the

Jimmy they knew of old.

'CHAKA-CHAKA-CHAKA-CHAKA-CHAKA!' Jimmy's voice rang harsh and cruel around the pickling laboratory. 'Boys,' he said to Thug and Slasher, 'forget Cheddar. I think we might be in for a good cat-crushing tonight. Take a look at this.'

Ginger Biscuit padded over to an old TV monitor and switched it on.

The three magpies crowded round. What they saw was Ricardo Butteredsconi, Pork and Zenia upstairs in the drawing room scoffing pickled chocolates. Butteredsconi muttered something to Pork. The pig trotted off and returned with the remote control in his mouth. The remote control had two security settings. It was currently set to PRETEND. Ricardo Butteredsconi's fat sausage fingers gripped the dial.

'Chaka-chaka-chaka-chaka-chaka!' the mapgies chattered their approval as Ricardo Butteredsconi slowly twisted it to the other setting: FOR REAL.

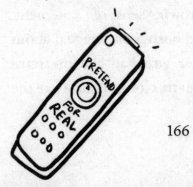

'There it is!' Mrs Tucker roared towards Butteredsconi's Pickle Factory on her motorbike.

Atticus and Mimi were squashed up in the sidecar with Michael and Callie. Mrs Cheddar perched behind Mrs Tucker on the seat.

Atticus turned his head. The ugly square factory loomed towards them out of the darkness. Beyond it, out to sea, Fort Sconi was just visible in the weak moonlight; pinpricks of electric light shone from the second-floor window, illuminating the rocks beneath.

Atticus looked apprehensively at the sky. It was a dark, windy night. Heavy clouds scudded across the moon. There was going to be a storm.

The motorbike skidded to a halt. Mrs Tucker removed her night-vision binoculars from her basket and swept the sea with them. 'Herman's not there yet,' she muttered. 'I hope he hurries up.'

Atticus did too. The plan was that Mr Tucker and Bones would provide backup in *The Jolly Jellyfish*. The rest of them would enter Fort Sconi via the tunnel under the sea. With any luck they would be able to rescue Inspector Cheddar and make their getaway before Butteredsconi and his gang even realised they were there.

Mrs Tucker got back on the motorbike. They sped towards the factory gates.

'They're locked!' Callie said.

The gates were chained and padlocked together.

Atticus hopped out. He might not be a cat burglar any more but the world's greatest cat detective could still open a padlock in an emergency. He picked at the lock carefully with his claws.

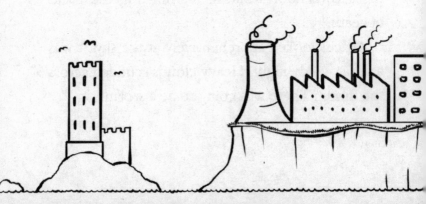

CLICK! The padlock sprung open.

'Well done, Atticus!' Michael said. He unwrapped the chain and pushed the factory gates open.

Mrs Tucker wheeled the motorbike into the shadows. 'We need to watch out for security cameras!' she hissed.

The rescuers crept through the gates.

Michael led the way to the corrugated door. Atticus hung back. He didn't want to go on the pickle ride again.

'Please, Atticus,' Callie pointed to a second padlock. 'Help us.'

Atticus swallowed his fear. Mrs Tucker held him up while he picked the second lock. This one was tougher than the padlock on the gates. His claws ached as he twisted the mechanism this way and that. Eventually the padlock gave way. Callie gave him a squeeze and kissed his paw better. 'Thank you, Atticus,' she whispered.

Mrs Tucker punched the button on the wall. The corrugated door rolled upwards.

They were in!

'Don't put the light on,' Mrs Tucker warned. 'We'll use torches.'

Everyone got out torches, except Atticus and Mimi who could see in the dark.

An empty cart shaped like a giant gherkin trundled along the track in front of them and came to a stop.

'Is it safe?' Mrs Tucker asked.

Callie nodded. 'It's just a ride about making pickles.'

'It's all fake,' Michael reassured Mrs Tucker. 'Don't worry.'

'Let's go, then.'

The kids jumped in the front. Mrs Cheddar went behind them. Mrs Tucker sat in the rear.

Atticus hesitated. Everything looked just the same as it had before, but his instinct screamed at him that something was wrong.

'What's up?' Mimi asked.

Atticus shook his head. 'It's all too easy. Butteredsconi and the villains must know that we might try and get in through the tunnel.'

'You think it's a trap?'

Just then the gherkin started to move.

'Come on, Atticus!' Callie called softly.

'Hurry up, Mimi!' Mrs Cheddar held out a hand.

'I guess we'll just have to risk it.' Atticus squeezed in between the children. Mimi jumped in with Mrs Cheddar.

CLANG! The bars clanged shut. The cart trundled forward. They were off.

Let me take you on a journey,' the voice of Ricardo Butteredsconi boomed around the secret tunnel, 'into the world of pickles.'

It was time for the flying meat. 'Duck!' Callie shouted.

Everyone ducked. BAMPH! Somehow they managed to twist to one side as the first huge lump of grizzly meat projected out at them from one side of the cart. BOOMPH! They twisted the other way as the second lump zoomed towards them from the other side of the tunnel.

BOOSH! The two joints of meat met in the middle, showering everyone with blood and gristle.

'I thought you said it was fake!' Mrs Tucker shouted from behind.

'It was!' Michael yelled back.

'Well this looks pretty realistic to me!' Mrs Tucker shouted.

171

Atticus felt afraid. His instinct had been right. The ride *was* different in one vital respect. Everything that happened to them when they first visited the factory was about to happen again, only this time it was for real!

Mrs Cheddar had worked it out too. 'Move to the back, kids!' she yelled.

'We can't!' Callie and Michael struggled with the bar.

'Imagine you are a piece of meat,' the voice intoned. 'About to be pickled.'

The meat had retreated to the wall.

'First, you would be washed with water.' The voice came again.

'Hold your breath!' Mrs Cheddar cried.

A deluge of water hit them in the face. Michael and Callie coughed and spluttered. So did Atticus and Mimi.

'Atticus?' Mimi meowed. She sounded petrified.

'Just do as Mrs Cheddar says!' Atticus meowed back. 'You'll be safe with her.'

'Then you would be rubbed with salt,' said the voice.

'Close your eyes!' Mrs Cheddar gasped. 'And

don't be scared if something grabs you from behind. That part of it won't be real.'

Atticus hoped she was right.

A blizzard of white crystals fell from the ceiling, covering them with salt.

CLUNK! Something gripped his shoulders. Callie screamed. So did Mrs Tucker. Six pairs of disembodied rubber hands kneaded their shoulders.

'You've got to get off the seat, kids!' Mrs Cheddar shouted again.

Atticus's heart raced. The blade was coming soon.

'Do it now!'

Callie and Michael twisted and wriggled. They slid off the seat into the foot well of the cart. Atticus was about to follow them when the bar tightened. It gripped him across the chest so tightly that he could hardly breathe.

'And then you would be left in the cold for several weeks,' the voice boomed.

Atticus braced himself. A blast of Arctic air hit him in the face like an iced brick. Atticus felt his whiskers freeze.

'Until you were ready to be carved.'

Atticus wriggled desperately. He knew the blade wouldn't miss this time. He had to escape!

'Unscrew the bar, Atticus,' Callie's frantic voice came from the foot well. 'Use your claws. Then we can push it up.'

Atticus turned his head. The bar was screwed on to each side of the cart with three round screws. One of them looked slightly loose. If he could loosen it a bit more then he might still have a chance. Squirming frantically, he managed to free his left paw. It wasn't the one he usually used, but he would have to manage somehow. He popped out his claws and reached for the loose screw. He bent his paw and fixed the back of his claw along the thread.

Slowly, painfully, he turned the screw once, twice, three times.

He could hear the blade descending.

Callie and Michael were pushing at the bar. It rocked slightly, but not enough for him to wriggle through.

'Once more, Atticus,' Michael urged.

The blade was perilously close.

Atticus turned the screw again. Four times. Five times. His claw ached with pain.

The two children heaved on the bar. He felt it give a little more.

'Atticus!' Mimi meowed. 'It's coming! Move!'

SWISH!

With one final squirm Atticus managed to twist himself free of the bar. He slid out from under it and collapsed on to the floor beside Callie and Michael, panting. But there was no time to rest.

'Now imagine you're a cucumber . . .'

Atticus tried to remember what came next.

'First you would be sliced into thin strips . . .'

Atticus heard the swish of the blade returning. 'Keep down,' Mrs Cheddar yelled.

The tunnel was becoming unbearably hot and smelly.

'Keep your eyes closed, Mimi!' Atticus meowed.

'What's happening now?' Mrs Tucker cried from behind.

'We're about to be pickled in vinegar!' Mrs Cheddar shouted.

'Not if I've got anything to do with it, we're not!'

Atticus couldn't see what Mrs Tucker was doing but it sounded as though she was rummaging in her basket again.

'Put these on!' Three plastic bags landed in the foot well of the cart. Atticus read the label.

THUMPERS'
Ginormous plastic mac
Keeps you dry even in the worst
weather conditions
(Also works with vinegar showers)

The children tore the bags open. They pulled on the plastic macs. Atticus waited patiently while they fitted him into his cat-sized one.

SPLOOSH! The vinegar washed over them in a stinking wave.

'And placed in sealed jars . . .'

Atticus looked up. The cart was wedged between the two sides of a giant burger bun.

'I can't breathe!' Callie gasped. She lifted her head to try to get some air.

'Stay down, Callie!' Mrs Cheddar shouted. 'It's nearly over.'

Michael pulled his sister down.

'Until it's time to be eaten with a burger and chips.'

Atticus visualised the enormous set of teeth filling the tunnel ahead of them. CHOMP! The cart rocked slightly as the teeth bit down. If they had remained in their seats the teeth would have chewed what was left of them.

'And that,' the voice said, 'completes our journey. But remember, the ancient art of pickling isn't just used on food.' The voice paused. The cats huddled together, listening. 'It is also a way to preserve BODIES, BODIES, BODIES, BODIES, BODIES . . .'

The cart jolted to a halt.

Atticus was about to hop out when he heard Mrs Tucker hiss, 'Keep down, everyone!'

He lowered his head smartly.

'My guess is we're on CCTV,' Mrs Tucker whispered. 'We'll lie low

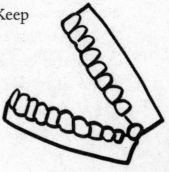

for a few minutes and let them think we've been pickled. Then we'll go and find your dad.'

Atticus hunkered down with Callie and Michael and waited.

'Where'd they go?' Thug said.

In the mortuary the three magpies were watching the TV monitor. They couldn't see everything that happened on the ride, only the bit where the intruders stepped on and off the gherkin cart. They had seen the humans and the cats step on. But they didn't step off.

'They're dead.' Ginger Biscuit switched off the monitor. 'Vroom, squish-squash, chomp! Just like we planned, only a bit ahead of schedule and with a giant set of teeth instead of a car.'

'But I never got to make a nest-snuggler,' Thug protested.

'Cheer up, Thug,' Slasher said. 'Just think: you can *buy* a nest snuggler with all the shiny things we'll nick when we get back to Littleton-on-Sea now that Claw's not around to stop us; or Inspector Cheese, for that matter. Now let's get this over with so we can get out of here.'

Squeak . . . squeak . . . squeak . . . squeak!

Just then the door to the mortuary opened. Zenia Klob appeared, pushing a hospital wheelie trolley covered in a white sheet. She was wearing her surgeon's disguise – a green scrub suit, a surgical mask and a pair of rubber boots. Ricardo Butteredsconi followed her in with Pork. Butteredsconi was dressed in the same fashion as Zenia, except that his scrub suit was made of the finest Italian silk.

Pork took a seat beside the drainage bucket, where he could get a good view. Pam fluttered down on to his ear and nibbled it affectionately. 'I love a good pickling!' she said. 'Don't you?'

Pork grunted.

The magpies fluttered on to a shelf and turned away.

'I can't watch,' Thug said.

'Me neither,' Slasher echoed.

'For once I actually agree with you,' Jimmy said.

'I can,' Ginger Biscuit sat beneath them on a bench. 'I just don't think I will, that's all.' He lay down and closed his eyes.

'CHICKENS!' Pam squawked in disgust. 'PUCK-PUCK-PUCK-PUCK-PUCK!'

Ginger Biscuit growled. 'I'll get her later,' he muttered.

Zenia pulled back the sheet.

Inspector Cheddar lay upon the trolley, snoring peacefully.

'Finally my dream has come true, Pork,' Ricardo Butteredsconi whispered. 'It is time to for us to create the greatest work of art the world has ever seen: a pickled human.' He pulled on a pair of white surgical gloves. 'Shall we?' he said to Zenia.

'Yes, let's!'' she giggled.

The two of them picked up the Inspector and transferred him to the shining mortuary table.

'All right, let's go,' Mrs Tucker said.

The rescuers let themselves out of their hiding place in the gherkin cart. They tiptoed across the arrival platform, keeping low in case a surveillance camera picked them up.

'This way!' Mrs Tucker hopped on to the travelator. The others followed.

'Are you all right?' Atticus asked Mimi.

She managed a weak purr. 'I'm fine. I just hope we don't have to do that on the way back!'

'Don't worry, the ride's only one way,' Atticus reassured her.

The travelator arrived into a great hall. Atticus looked about. There were no windows and the air was cold. They must be beneath the sea.

The hall was stuffed with priceless stolen works of art. Paintings covered every inch of the walls. The floor was scattered with sculpture, including *The Camp Bed*. The bed was just as Atticus remembered it before Inspector Cheddar got into it – with the carelessly folded pyjamas and the half-drunk cup of tea. But there was no sign of the Inspector; the villains had taken him somewhere else.

'That's the missing Pollock,' Mrs Cheddar said, pointing to a huge painting. Atticus glanced at it – the canvas was a magical splurge of colour splashed with thick splots and drizzles of paint. 'And that's

the *Mona Lisa*. And there's Atticus's painting of Littleton-on-Sea.'

The beach scene was sandwiched between the others. It was *okay*, Atticus thought, pausing to take a quick look, but he still had a lot to learn, especially from Pollock.

'Atticus!' Mrs Tucker hissed. 'Stop gawping at the paintings and hurry up!'

They dashed through into the next room. It was even bigger than the last.

'That's gross,' Callie said.

Table upon table was crowded with jars, pots, bottles, and clear plastic tubs. Around the room, shelves were piled high with vases and beakers and jugs. Strewn across the floor, assorted glass tanks of all different shapes and sizes jostled for space.

All of them contained animals.

'Butteredsconi's pickled art collection,' Michael whispered.

Atticus regarded it with horror. There were (as you have probably already guessed) bats, rats, gnats, lizards, monkeys, mice, lice, spiders, snakes, drakes, goats, stoats, moles, voles, scorpions, millipedes, zillipedes, trillipedes, hogs, frogs, loads of toads, quails, snails, baby whales, sows, cows, bugs, pugs, slugs, weevils, beavers, chicks, ticks, foxes, oxes, germs, worms, bees, fleas and manatees . . . and, of course, sharks, including the megalodon, which stretched from one end of the room to the other in an enormous glass tank. The animals stared blindly back at Atticus like the faces from his dream.

'Come on,' Mrs Tucker said urgently.

They picked their way across the crowded floor.

The next room was different. You couldn't really call it a room, Atticus decided. It was a viewing gallery. A steel platform ran around the edge of a glass tank. He scampered on to the platform and peered through the glass. The tank was full of a clear liquid with a bluish tinge. It stank of chemicals. Apart from that it was empty.

'What's that for?' Michael asked.

Atticus glanced at Mrs Cheddar. Her face was white. She *knew*.

'It's for Dad,' said a small voice. It was Callie's. 'Isn't it, Mum? That's why they've kept him prisoner. They're going to pickle him and put him in Mr Butteredsconi's art collection.'

Mrs Cheddar nodded dumbly.

'I'd like to see them try!' Mrs Tucker fumed. 'We'll stop them, won't we, Atticus?'

Atticus meowed his agreement. He would do anything – ANYTHING – to save Inspector Cheddar and help his family.

'We need to find out where Butteredsconi's pickling laboratory is,' Mrs Tucker said.

Atticus looked carefully round the room. If you wanted to catch a villain you had to think like one. Butteredsconi and the gang planned to put Inspector Cheddar in the tank once they'd pickled him, which meant there had to be a way to get to the tank from the pickling laboratory. Atticus soon saw what he was looking for. Opposite them, on the other side of the steel platform, was a lift. He scampered across it, meowing, his claws clattering on the metal.

'Good work, Atticus,' Mrs Tucker and the others hurried over.

'The pickling laboratory's in the basement!' Mrs Cheddar cried. She pressed the button.

The lift descended. The doors opened. The rescuers peeped out cautiously. They must be well below sea level now, Atticus thought, in a part of the fort that Butteredsconi hadn't renovated since the mad doctor lived there. The walls were lined with chipped green tiles. Single light bulbs dangled at intervals from the ceiling. The floor was damp and uneven.

Atticus sniffed. He could smell magpie. He flattened his ears and hissed.

'Follow Atticus,' Mrs Tucker ordered. 'He's on to something.'

Atticus padded cautiously along the musty corridor. They passed a door marked ELECTRICITY: KEEP OUT and another with a sign over it which said DISPENSARY.

'What's a dis-pen-sar-y?' Callie whispered,

sounding the word out carefully.

'It's where you make medicines,' Mrs Tucker told her.

'We'd better go and have a look,' Mrs Cheddar said. 'There might be something in there that can help us.'

'Okay.' Callie and Michael squeezed their way into the little room with their mum. Atticus heard the *ting* of bottles.

He padded on along the corridor with Mimi; Mrs Tucker removed her boots and tiptoed behind them.

Atticus pricked up his ears. He could hear voices coming from a room to his right. Bright light shone from it into the corridor. The door was wedged open by a rubber doorstop. Above the doorframe the word MORTUARY had been crossed out and replaced by the words PICKLING LABORATORY.

Mrs Tucker knelt down. She took out a periscope from her basket and poked it round the door. 'Oh my giddy aunt,' she said.

The two cats took turns to look through it.

Inspector Cheddar lay on a gleaming metal slab. To one side

of him was a large basin. To the other was a copper cylinder labelled FORMALDEHYDE. Behind the mortuary slab Zenia Klob was in the process of selecting a hypodermic needle from a tray placed upon the bench. Ricardo Butteredsconi was fiddling with the tubes from the cylinder.

Pam and Pork had ringside seats close by. Pam was on Pork's head. The two of them were watching Zenia closely.

Atticus held his breath: they were only a few metres away from Pork, but Pork was so engrossed in the gruesome spectacle before him that he hadn't noticed the new smell of cat. Or perhaps it was because everything in the mortuary stank of chemicals.

Zenia held up a needle to the light. 'Vot about this vun?'

Butteredsconi looked up. 'Too small!' he said.

Zenia turned back the instrument tray.

'This one?'

'Too big.' He gestured at the tank. 'It needs to be just right so that we can pump it into his bloodstream nice and slowly.'

Atticus felt his hackles rise.

'They're going to replace Inspector Cheddar's blood with formaldehyde!' Mrs Tucker whispered. 'We need to think of something. Fast!'

22

Atticus felt a hand on his head. He jumped.

'It's all right, Atticus, it's just us,' Callie said soothingly.

Callie, Michael and Mrs Cheddar squatted down beside Mrs Tucker.

'We found these,' Michael said. He placed a dusty glass bottle of Vita-Vit liquid vitamins and a faded cardboard carton of Sleepy-Snooze smelling salts on the floor.

'I'm not sure they're much help,' Mrs Cheddar said anxiously, 'although some vitamins might do him good.'

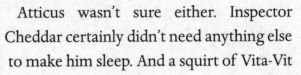

Atticus wasn't sure either. Inspector Cheddar certainly didn't need anything else to make him sleep. And a squirt of Vita-Vit probably wouldn't be enough to bring him round, even if they could think of a way of getting it into him!

Think! he told himself. *Think!*

Just then the electric lights flickered. BOOM! The sound of thunder rumbled in the distance. The storm had struck.

Inspector Cheddar stirred slightly in his sleep. He gave a little moan. 'Ooaaaa . . . Ooooaaaaaaa . . .'

The sound of chattering erupted from somewhere at the back of the mortuary. 'Chaka-chaka-chaka-chaka-chaka . . .'

The magpies! Atticus peeped through the periscope. His eyes swept the room. *There!* He pinpointed the three birds, huddled together on a shelf. Ginger Biscuit sat beneath them on the bench. He made an angry swipe at the magpies. They were teasing him about something. Atticus strained his ears to listen.

'It's like one of them horror films,' Thug chattered.

'Yeah,' Slasher agreed. 'It's the same as what happened to that Dr Frankenstein bloke. I'll bet when Butteredsconi pumps him full of pickle juice he turns nasty and starts mangling us.'

'Shut up.' Ginger Biscuit took another swipe.

'He'll pull all your whiskers out in a minute,' Thug predicted. 'Just you wait.'

'Grrrrrrr . . .'

Atticus felt a shiver of excitement. He'd had the beginnings of an idea. If Ginger Biscuit was afraid of Inspector Cheddar, then the other villains might be too.

From outside there was another clap of thunder.

The electric lights flickered again.

Inspector Cheddar gave a snort. 'Mwhhhhhhooo,' he groaned.

Zenia paused in her needle selection. She looked round, frowning.

Atticus's eyes gleamed. Zenia didn't like it either. The idea was taking shape in his mind.

'Should I give him another shot of sleeping potion?' she said to Butteredsconi.

Ricardo Butteredsconi nodded.

Zenia reached under her surgical hat for a hairpin. 'Curses,' she swore, 'I left them upstairs. I'll go and get them.'

'No!' Ricardo Butteredsconi's voice rang round the mortuary. 'We do not have time for that. We will complete the pickling now.'

Zenia gave him a sharp look. 'Very vell, Ricardo,' she said. 'If you insist.' She turned back to the instruments.

'That's it then,' Thug remarked dolefully. 'I wouldn't be surprised if Inspector Cheese rips our heads off with his bare hands.'

'Not *our* heads, Thug,' Slasher objected. 'I mean, it wasn't our idea to pickle him. Zenia's head, more like. And Butteredsconi's, obviously . . .'

'And Pork's,' Thug said.

'And Pam's,' Jimmy put in.

'And Biscuit's,' Slasher suggested.

'Why mine?' Ginger Biscuit snarled. 'I haven't done anything.'

'Yeah you did!' Thug said. 'You helped steal him from the art gallery.'

'So did you!'

'He didn't *see* us, though,' Thug retorted. 'Just you and Zenia.'

Ginger Biscuit growled.

Atticus knew now what they had to do. The

Vita-Vit might just work, especially if they gave Inspector Cheddar a huge squirt. For once he felt grateful to the magpies. It was they who had planted the idea in his mind. If only he could explain it to the humans! For the second time that week Atticus wished that humans were as good at understanding Cat as cats were at understanding Human. *Oh well,* he thought, *I'll just have to try.*

Zenia made her final selection. 'This vun looks good.' She inserted the needle into a syringe and approached the slab. Her gnarly fingers reached for Inspector Cheddar's neck.

BOOM! The thunder struck again, closer this time. The lights flickered for a few seconds.

Inspector Cheddar started to gurgle in between snores. It was a horrible noise, somewhere between a slurp and a slobber. 'Get off me!' he said, twisting his neck so that his chin got in the way of Zenia's probing fingers. He batted at the syringe with a floppy arm. It clattered to the floor and rolled under the mortuary table.

'Curses.' Zenia bent down to look for it. 'He's vaking up!'

194

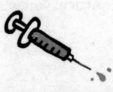

Atticus saw his chance. He nudged the bottle of Thumpers' Vita-Vit towards the children with his paw.

'You want to give some to Dad?' Callie guessed.

'But what good will it do?' asked Mrs Cheddar.

Atticus staggered about stiffly, pulling a horrible face. Then he put his tail between his legs and ran off down the corridor, pretending to be Ginger Biscuit.

'I get it now. It's to scare the villains off, isn't it?!' Michael's face glowed with excitement. 'Like Frankenstein! If Dad wakes up a bit they'll think he's turning into a monster and run away?'

Atticus brushed his tail against the children and purred throatily to show them they were right.

'That's brilliant!' Mrs Tucker said, giving him a cat treat from her pocket.

'Here, you'll need one of these.' She reached into her basket. 'Mind you don't prick yourself.' She handed a syringe to Michael. It had a sharp needle on the end.

'Let me guess.' He grinned, pulling open the cellophane wrapping carefully. 'Standard MI6 kit?'

'Of course,' Mrs Tucker said. 'All Atticus needs to do is switch the syringes.' She got up. 'I'll go and turn off the electricity; that will really freak the freaks out. And it will give Atticus some cover.' She tiptoed back towards the cupboard.

Callie took the glass stopper from the bottle of Vita-Vit. Michael held the bottle while Mrs Cheddar drew a large measure of the vitamin liquid into the syringe.

Atticus looked on. 'Will you help me?' he asked Mimi.

'Yes.' Mimi nodded.

The lights went out.

'Vot's going on?' Zenia's voice cried from the mortuary.

'Whooaaaaaa!' Inspector Cheddar was moaning again.

'Get on with it!' Butteredsconi shouted.

'Chaka-chaka-chaka-chaka-chaka!' the magpies chattered in alarm.

'Here it is!' Mrs Cheddar held out the syringe to Atticus.

Atticus took it carefully in his mouth.

'Follow me,' he said to Mimi, only it came out more as, 'Foom', because he had a syringe full of Thumpers' Vita-Vit between his teeth.

The two cats crept round the door into the mortuary.

Zenia Klob was groping about on the floor, feeling for the dropped syringe. 'It's here somevere!' Zenia shrieked. 'Ah, here ve are!'

'Oh no ve're not!' Mimi dashed over and swept the syringe out of the way with her paw.

Atticus bounded after Mimi. He placed the syringe with Vita-Vit as close as he dared to Zenia's grasping hand.

The two cats retreated to the door.

'Found it!' Zenia gripped it triumphantly. She got to her feet.

'You get the tube, Ricardo,' she said, 'vile I stick this in his neck. Then ve can start the pump.'

Ricardo Butteredsconi grasped the tube.

CTSSSHHHHH . . .

Zenia raised the syringe full of Vita-Vit and plunged it into Inspector Cheddar's jugular.

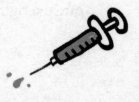

A limp human leg swung over the side of the mortuary table, followed by another.

'Whooaaaaa!'

'It's working,' Michael whispered.

Inspector Cheddar stood up.

A flash of lightning illuminated the pickling laboratory.

'Oh dear,' said Mrs Cheddar. 'I think I might have used a bit too much Vita-Vit. It's stronger than I thought.'

Atticus's fur prickled. Inspector Cheddar was a terrible sight. His green hair stood on end. His eyes were glazed. The hypodermic needle stuck out at a right angle from his neck. His head jerked this way and that. Slowly he raised his arms and started to walk forward. 'Mmmmmmwwwwwhhh hhhhhoooooooooaaaaaaaaaaahhhhhhhh . . . '

The villains retreated to the edge of the laboratory, all except Pork and Pam, who stood their ground.

'STOP! STOP! STOP! STOP! STOP!' Pam shrieked.

Pork bared his yellow teeth.

Inspector Cheddar lashed out with one leg. The two animals sailed through the air.

SQUAWK! Pam landed in the drainage bucket.

CRASH! Pork landed on top of her.

'The Vita-Vit's given Dad super strength!' Michael said in awe.

'It must have reacted with Zenia's sleeping potion!' Mrs Tucker whistled. 'Whatever happens, keep out of his way,' she advised.

CRASH! BUMP! BASH! Inspector Cheddar swept his dangling arms along the laboratory shelves. Needles and test tubes rained down, together with lots of bottles and surgical instruments, three magpies and a large ginger cat. 'Mmmmwwwwhhhoooooaaaaaaa!'

Zenia grabbed hold of Biscuit. 'Come here, my furry fiend.'

Biscuit didn't protest. Atticus could see he was terrified.

'Chaka-chaka-chaka-chaka-chaka!' The magpies picked themselves up and flapped out of the mortuary. They were in such a hurry to escape they didn't see the rescuers crouching in the shadows.

'Which way now, Boss?' Thug screeched.

'This way.' Jimmy led them along the corridor in the opposite direction from the lift.

Suddenly a terrifying figure appeared in front of them. It had long hair and a huge beard-jumper. Its tatty clothes were splattered with disgusting-smelling dung. It limped out of the darkness with a great roar.

'Another monster!' Thug screamed. The magpies flapped back the other way.

'Herman!' Mrs Tucker exclaimed. 'About time! Where did you come from?'

'We's got in from the landing stage through the sewers,' Mr Tucker said. 'That's why I smells like a pig's faaarrrrrt.'

Bones hopped out of Mr Tucker's jacket. Luckily it had kept her dry and she still smelled of the pet spa treatment, not pig fart.

'What's going on, Edna?' Mr Tucker demanded.

CRASH! BASH! SMASH! Inspector Cheddar was still smashing up the pickling laboratory.

Mrs Tucker quickly explained the situation. 'Whatever you do, don't go near him. The combination of the Vita-Vit and Zenia's sleeping potion seems to be pretty toxic. He's in some kind of a super-strength trance.'

'We'll round up the magpies. Come on, Bones.' Mimi charged off down the corridor with Bones.

Just then Ricardo Butteredsconi squeezed through the doorway from the pickling laboratory and stumbled towards the lift.

'Mmmmwwwwhhhhhooooaaaaa!' Inspector Cheddar wasn't far behind him.

'Run!' Mrs Tucker yelled. Everyone ran for cover.

Suddenly Atticus remembered the Sleepy-Snooze Smelling Salts. He grabbed the cardboard packet in his teeth.

BASH, SMASH, CRASH! Inspector Cheddar

was getting into the lift. There was no sign of Butteredsconi.

'He must have gone up the stairs!' Mrs Tucker cried. 'Come on!'

They raced up the emergency stairs. Mrs Tucker shouldered her way through the heavy fire door into the viewing gallery.

Ricardo Butteredsconi was edging backwards along the metal platform that surrounded the pickling tank, his piggy eyes fixed on Inspector Cheddar.

The Inspector looked even more terrible in the bright light of the gallery. His veins bulged. His green hair was wilder than ever. And his eyeballs were sticking out. 'Mmmmmhhhhhhhrrrrrrrr!' he groaned.

'No! Please!' Butteredsconi knees gave way. He collapsed against the glass barrier.

Inspector Cheddar took a swipe at him.

SPLASH!

'Help me, someone!' Butteredsconi bobbed about helplessly in the pickle tank, waving his arms above him. 'I can't swim.'

'Fish him out, Herman!' Mrs Tucker shouted.

Mr Tucker produced a fishing rod from his pocket and hooked the pickle giant by the tie. 'Shall I bash him on the head with me basher?' he asked as he reeled him in.

'No, just tie him up,' Mrs Tucker ordered.

'Mum!' Callie shouted. 'Mrs Tucker! Quick! Dad's going to destroy the art!'

CRASH! BASH! SMASH! In the next room Inspector Cheddar was already making short work of Ricardo Butteredsconi's pickled animal collection.

'What are we going to do?' Michael cried.

'We can't get near him,' Mrs Tucker said. 'It's too dangerous. We'll just have to wait for the Vita-Vit to wear off.'

'But the art . . .' Callie began.

'No, Callie,' Mrs Tucker said firmly.

Mimi rushed up. 'Is there anything *we* can do to stop him?' she said to Atticus.

Atticus put the cardboard packet of Thumpers' Sleepy-Snooze down carefully. 'Maybe,' he said. 'Where are the magpies?'

'Here!' Bones stepped forwards, pulling a net full of black and white feathers.

'Claw!' Jimmy snarled. 'I . . .'

Atticus held up a paw. 'I know. You're going to peck my eyes out and make me into a nest snuggler. Look, Jimmy. I haven't got time for all that. I need your help.'

'Whatd'esay?' Thug spluttered.

'You kidding me?' Slasher coughed.

'I want to call a truce.'

Mimi and Bones looked at Atticus in amazement.

'A truce?' Jimmy eyed him suspiciously.

'I want you to take this box,' Atticus pointed to the Sleepy-Snooze Smelling Salts, 'and sprinkle it on top of Inspector Cheddar.' He paused. 'Then you're free to go. I promise.'

There was a brief silence.

'All right,' Jimmy Magpie said at length. 'But this isn't over, Claw. We'll get our revenge on you one day. You'd better watch your back.'

'Yeah!' Thug and Slasher's beady eyes were on him. 'You heard the boss!'

'We'll get you!'

'Sure you will,' Atticus said. He slashed through the net with a sharp claw. The magpies hopped out. Atticus pushed the packet of Sleepy-Snooze towards them. 'Now do it before I change my mind,' he growled. 'It's hungry work catching criminals, isn't it, girls?'

'It sure is!' Mimi and Bones meowed. Three pairs of gleaming cats' eyes bore down on the magpies.

With a final evil stare at Atticus, Jimmy Magpie grabbed the packet of Sleepy-Snooze in his beak. The three magpies took off.

'Look!' Callie said. 'Atticus has let the magpies go!'

'They've got the Sleepy-Snooze,' Michael said.

'Atticus must have made a deal with them,' Mrs Tucker whistled. 'He's one clever cat.'

'Are you sure you did the right thing?' Bones whispered.

'I don't know,' Atticus admitted. 'But I wanted to try to save the art.'

SMASH! CRASH! BASH!

Mimi squeezed his paw. 'Whatever happens, Atticus, I'm proud of you,' she said.

The cats made their way through the remains of the pickled animals into the great hall with the children and the grown-ups.

Atticus could hardly bear to look. He didn't

mind if Inspector Cheddar stamped on his painting of Littleton-on-Sea. He could always do another one. *But what if the Pollock is ruined? Or the* Mona Lisa? *Or all those beautiful statues?* They were like the megalodon; there would never be another one of them ever again in the whole entire world. And that, he knew, would be terrible for everyone who never got the chance to look at them and see things differently, like he had. He closed his eyes.

BASH! CRASH! SMASH!

SMASH! CRASH! BASH!

'CHAKA-CHAKA-CHAKA-CHAKA-CHAKA!'

Suddenly everything went quiet apart from a gentle sound of snoring.

'It's all right, Atticus,' Mimi said. 'The magpies did it. The art is safe.'

Atticus opened one eye, then the other.

Inspector Cheddar lay on *The Camp Bed*, sleeping peacefully, surrounded by the fabulous, priceless art. Beside him lay the empty box of Sleepy-Snooze Smelling Salts.

There was no sign of Jimmy Magpie and his gang. They had gone.

24

'So what happened then?'

Back in Littleton-on-Sea Atticus was telling the story to the kittens at the local cats' home. One of them, whose name was Thomas, was so excited by the whole adventure he'd fallen off his cushion.

'Mrs Tucker called the Commissioner. The police came in a launch and arrested Butteredsconi and Pork. The two of them are in jail.' Atticus's whiskers twitched in amusement. 'I've heard they don't like the food very much.'

Mrs Tucker had put them on a diet of bread and water.

'What happened to Zenia Klob?' another kitten asked. 'And Ginger Biscuit?'

'Unfortunately they escaped,' Atticus said.

'They must have hidden in the sewers until Mr Tucker and Bones were out of the way and then escaped on the hover-boat. Interpol think they're back in Siberia.'

'And Pam?' Thomas asked.

Atticus sighed. 'Pam is in intensive care at Her Majesty's Prison for Bad Birds,' he told them. 'Pork flattened her with his rump cheek when he fell on top of her. The vets are trying to re-inflate her with a bicycle pump.' Jimmy Magpie would be pleased anyway, he thought.

Atticus glanced at the clock. Callie and Michael would be here soon with Mrs Cheddar to pick him up. The vet had signed him off sick for three weeks with a sprained paw.

'Is Inspector Cheddar all right?' Thomas asked.

'He's as all right as he's ever been, I suppose,' Atticus grumbled. Atticus had injured his paw undoing the padlocks. It was all bandaged up. But Inspector Cheddar seemed to have forgotten his own advice about the need to elevate sprained limbs, and kept telling him to get off the sofa at home. Atticus almost liked him better when he was a monster.

'Do you know where the magpies are?' another kitten asked.

'No, but I've got an idea that they'll be back causing trouble before too long,' Atticus said cheerfully. 'They've always wanted to return to their nest under the pier.'

'Don't you mind?' Thomas frowned.

'Not really,' Atticus said. 'It was worth letting them go to save the art. And it'll give Inspector Cheddar something to do if they go on another crime spree. He's running around giving everyone speeding tickets at the moment, even if they're on a bike. The doctor said the Vita-Vit would take a while to wear off.'

'Will you be doing any more painting?' another kitten said.

'Definitely!' Atticus replied. 'Which reminds me, Callie and Michael have got a surprise for you.'

The Cheddars' Ford Focus pulled up outside. Mrs Cheddar got out with the children and Mimi. Zeberdee Cronk was with them. They hurried into the cats' home with lots of bags.

'We've brought some painting stuff,' Callie explained to the kittens. 'We thought you might like to do some paw prints.'

'Yeah, cat art is the new cool!' Michael said.

'Meow! Meow! Meow!' The kittens followed the children into the kitchen.

'Hey!' Zeberdee greeted Atticus. 'How are you doing?'

Atticus purred contentedly. He was fine, apart from his paw.

'I was thinking I might take you to visit a few more galleries,' Zeberdee said. 'Would you like that?'

Atticus purred throatily. He would love it.

'Your painting of the beach at Littleton-on-Sea looks great, by the way, in Tate Modern.'

Atticus was pleased. Mrs Cheddar had donated his painting to the gallery. He hoped people enjoyed looking at it as much as he'd enjoyed painting it.

Zeberdee picked him up carefully and took him into the kitchen with the others.

Atticus lay down in one of the kittens' baskets with Mimi next to him, watching the kittens do their paw prints. They chose all sorts of different colours: red and green and gold and blue, pink and purple and even turquoise. They all had a wonderful time.

'I like that one best,' Mimi pointed at Thomas's picture. 'I think it's supposed to be you.'

Atticus squinted at it.

It didn't look like him, but Atticus knew that didn't matter! It was black and brown, with a twist of white and a splodge of red in one corner.

'That's pretty good,' Atticus told Thomas, 'for a beginner.'

Thomas puffed out his chest with pride.

Callie picked the picture up. She grabbed a pen and wrote Thomas's name in one corner. Then she handed the pen to Michael and in the other corner, beneath the red splodge, he scribbled

Atticus Grammaticus

Cattypuss Claw

best cat in the world

Author's Note

This book owes a lot to the brilliant imaginations of the artists who inspired it. Without Damien Hirst's pickled shark (*The Physical Impossibility of Death in the Mind of Someone Living*), Tracey Emin's iconic *My Bed* and Doris Salcedo's *Shibboleth* (the crack), Inspector Cheddar would not have been at risk of becoming the world's ultimate work of art at the hands of an obsessed art-collecting pickle giant and his greedy pet pig.

As you have probably already guessed, *Pacific Ocean*, *The Toenail Tree* and *Mount Underwear* are all my own creations, which no doubt explains why I am a writer and not an artist.

Many thanks to the editorial team at Faber for keeping me on track and giving me the opportunity to explore the world of art with Atticus.